Enrollment Form

☐ *Yes!* I WANT TO BE A *Privileged Woman.*

Enclosed is one *PAGES & PRIVILEGES*™ Proof of Purchase from any Harlequin or Silhouette book currently for sale in stores (Proofs of Purchase are found on the back pages of books) and the store cash register receipt. Please enroll me in *PAGES & PRIVILEGES*™. Send my Welcome Kit and FREE Gifts -- and activate my FREE benefits -- immediately.

More great gifts and benefits to come like these luxurious Truly Lace and L'Effleur gift baskets.

► DETACH HERE AND MAIL TODAY! ►

NAME (please print)

ADDRESS   APT. NO

CITY   STATE   ZIP/POSTAL CODE

PROOF OF PURCHASE
SAMPLE ONLY

Please allow 6-8 weeks for delivery. Quantities are limited. We reserve the right to substitute items. Enroll before October 31, 1995 and receive one full year of benefits.

NO CLUB!
NO COMMITMENT!
Just one purchase brings you great Free Gifts and Benefits!
(More details in back of this book.)

Name of store where this book was purchased_____

Date of purchase_____

Type of store:

☐ Bookstore   ☐ Supermarket   ☐ Drugstore

☐ Dept. or discount store (e.g. K-Mart or Walmart)

☐ Other (specify)_____

Which Harlequin or Silhouette series do you usually read?

Complete and mail with one Proof of Purchase and store receipt to:

U.S.: *PAGES & PRIVILEGES*™, P.O. Box 1960, Danbury, CT 06813-1960

Canada: *PAGES & PRIVILEGES*™, 49-6A The Donway West, P.O. 813, North York, ON M3C 2E8

PRINTED IN U.S.A

"It'll be nice to burrow beneath a quilt in front of a roaring fire during a winter storm,"

Raleigh suggested.

"Mmm," Dan said. "I can almost smell beef stew bubbling on the stove."

"And hear wind blowing." Raleigh grinned, her mind easily conjuring the cozy domestic scene.

"Playing cards…"

"Drinking hot chocolate with marshmallows…"

"Making love."

"Huh?" Raleigh's face flushed. "What did you say?"

"Making love," Dan repeated. "Isn't that one of the things people do in front of a warm fire on a frosty winter night?"

Dear Reader,

Ah, summertime…those lazy afternoons and sultry nights. The perfect time to find romance with a mysterious stranger in a far-off land, or right in your own backyard—with an irresistible Silhouette Romance hero. Like Nathan Murphy, this month's FABULOUS FATHER. Nathan had no interest in becoming a family man, but when Faith Reynolds's son, Cory, showed him *The Daddy List*, Nathan couldn't help losing his heart to the boy, and his pretty mom.

The thrills continue as two strong-willed men show their women how to trust in love. Elizabeth August spins a stirring tale for ALWAYS A BRIDESMAID! in *The Bridal Shower*. When Mike Flint heard that Emma Wynn was about to marry another man, he was determined to know if her love for him was truly gone, or burning deep within. In Laura Anthony's *Raleigh and the Rancher* for WRANGLERS AND LACE, ranch hand Raleigh Travers tries her best to resist ranch owner Daniel McClintock. Can Daniel's love help Raleigh forget her unhappy past?

Sometimes the sweetest passions can be found right next door, or literally on your doorstep, as in Elizabeth Sites's touching story *Stranger in Her Arms* and the fun-filled *Bachelor Blues* by favorite author Carolyn Zane.

Natalie Patrick makes her writing debut with the heartwarming *Wedding Bells and Diaper Pins*. Winning custody of her infant godson seemed a lost cause for Dani McAdams until ex-fiancé Matt Taylor offered a marriage of convenience. But unexpected feelings between them soon began to complicate their convenient arrangement!

Happy Reading!

Anne Canadeo
Senior Editor

Please address questions and book requests to:
Silhouette Reader Service
U.S.: 3010 Walden Ave., P.O. Box 1325, Buffalo, NY 14269
Canadian: P.O. Box 609, Fort Erie, Ont. L2A 5X3

RALEIGH AND THE RANCHER

Laura Anthony

Silhouette
ROMANCE™
Published by Silhouette Books
America's Publisher of Contemporary Romance

To my father, Fred Blalock, for instilling in me a love of
reading and a desire to write. And to my mother,
Maxine Reid Blalock, for giving me the courage and
determination to achieve my dream.

Special thanks to Mike Rountree for telling me all about
farriers.

 SILHOUETTE BOOKS

ISBN 0-373-19092-1

RALEIGH AND THE RANCHER

Copyright © 1995 by Laurie Blalock Moeller

LAURA ANTHONY

composed her first story at age eight and has been writing ever since. She entered nursing school when she was only seventeen and now, almost twenty years later, divides her time between nursing and writing romance. Born in West Texas, Laura currently resides on the banks of the Brazos River, surrounded by a forest filled with various critters. Her hobbies include boating, jogging and an occasional golf game with her husband, Tony.

Dear Reader,

There's something inherently romantic about cowboys. From their slow-talking drawl, to their strong, silent countenance, they exude a certain irresistible masculinity. And the modern cowboy is no less than his historical counterpart. They're hardworking, dedicated and highly principled men.

Growing up in West Texas, I was privy to many a tall tale about cowboys. I'd sit on the front porch listening to my daddy spin yarns of stalwart knights in buckskin who galloped on horseback across the prairie to salvage stray cattle, or who battled inclement weather, defeated dastardly villains and rescued lovely damsels. Daddy relayed exciting stories of untamed, independent men who blazed the early frontier, cared passionately for the land and left a legacy of honor that permeates Texas heritage to this day.

Raised on these stories, it was only natural that I turned to such fables for inspiration. I can only hope I've done justice to the legend.

Laura Anthony

Chapter One

Raleigh Travers needed a job—badly.

And now that she finally had a chance at one she had to look as competent for the position as possible. She'd dressed carefully in faded jeans, a navy blue, ribbed tank top and scuffed cowboy boots. Her copper-colored hair hung down her back in a thick, single braid, and she'd tied a red bandanna around her head to keep perspiration from her eyes. She was hoping her attire would reflect the tough, rugged image she wanted to portray.

Raleigh guided her battered brown pickup off the main highway and onto the graveled road. A chalky cloud of dust billowed beneath the worn tires as she goosed the reluctant vehicle up a steady incline.

Wind rushed in through the open window, whipping escaping tendrils of hair into her face. Flipping down the visor, she retrieved a pair of aviator sunglasses and pushed them up on her nose.

The sunglasses helped disguise her anxiety. She had to have this job! If she couldn't come up with the rent money soon, she and Caleb would be out on the street.

"Raleigh, you're going to have to do some tall talkin'," she said to her reflection in the rearview mirror.

Pa's pitiful insurance settlement was gone. During the previous six months she'd done her best to find work, but she'd been repeatedly turned down for countless jobs—jobs she was perfectly capable of performing. Even old friends and customers who knew she was a darn good farrier denied her a chance. They all said the same thing—she was too small, too young, too feminine to be doing a man's job.

Funny, no one had thought that way when she'd worked side by side with her father, shoeing horses from dawn until dusk, but then she'd just been Will Travers's tomboy daughter. Now, while she struggled to get her own business started, the townsfolk refused to take her seriously.

Over and over, she'd been advised to find work waiting tables or typing reports or watching children. Some even suggested she find a husband.

She snorted indelicately at that thought. With a younger brother to support, marriage was the last thing on her mind. Besides, she couldn't bear the pain of falling in love again. Immediately she thought of Jack and the awful events that had irrevocably altered her life. The familiar ache echoed inside her like lonely whispers in an empty dream.

Raleigh tossed her head. No. She would *not* relive past sorrows. Her future held more pressing concerns than self-pity. Gritting her teeth, she grasped the steering wheel tighter and thought of her upcoming interview. West of town a new owner had started renovations on a ramshackle horse ranch. She hoped to find the present management more receptive to a female farrier than the hardheaded, shortsighted citizens of Clyde, Texas.

Up ahead she could see the entrance to the ranch. Barbed wire gave way to white wooden corral fencing. Above the gateway hung a brand-new six-foot sign proclaiming McClintock Dude Ranch.

Dude ranch? In Clyde? Raleigh grinned. She hoped the newcomer's wallet matched his flair for farfetched fantasies. The cost of making this project work would not be cheap.

Bumping over the cattle guard, Raleigh lumbered onto the barren landscape of sagebrush, cactus, bull nettles, scrub oaks and yucca growing in untamed profusion. Aiming her pickup down the narrow rutted road, she rattled and jolted across the arid pasture, then pulled to a stop in the middle of a wide circular driveway.

The place was in the midst of recent reconstruction. Cement forms were tossed in haphazard heaps beside piles of mounded earth. Stacks of raw lumber decorated the rough terrain, and the smell of fresh paint lingered on the sultry breeze.

A large, two-story farmhouse hulked straight ahead. A bright red barn graced the hill to the right of the house. Next to it sat two stables, a small log cabin, probably meant for the ranch hands, an exercise yard and three separate corrals. Opposite the house sprawled a dilapidated swimming pool, deserted tennis courts and a faded shuffleboard slab.

A mix of Thoroughbreds and quarter horses grazed in the fields. Raleigh estimated their number at two dozen. Enough to net her over a thousand dollars.

She opened the pickup door and swung to the ground, her bootheels sinking into the yielding sand. Tucking her fingertips into her back pockets, she scanned the area.

Nobody in sight.

Stalking across the exercise yard, her braid bouncing between her shoulder blades, she hoped to appear self-confident despite the nervous perspiration coating her palms.

"Anybody home?" she called.

No answer.

Climbing over the corral, she stopped to scratch the nose of a friendly gelding Thoroughbred. "Hey, boy," she cooed. The horse nuzzled her arm in greeting.

"Where's your owner?" she asked the affectionate animal. Out of curiosity, she stooped over, lifted the Thoroughbred's right foreleg and examined his shoe. She clicked her tongue. The gelding drastically needed a new set.

"Hey, you! You there! What do you think you're doing?"

Raleigh's head snapped up.

The horse nickered. Dropping the animal's leg, she turned. Her sunglasses slipped down on her nose and she pushed them back up, squinting at the tall figure striding toward her.

Bushy eyebrows formed a frowning V on his wide forehead. A stubble of heavy beard enhanced his angular jaw. He wore tight jeans and a blue chambray work shirt with the sleeves rolled up, revealing hairy, muscular forearms. A black cowboy hat rode his head. He towered over her, obstructing her view of the sky. Broad of chest and thin of waist, he presented an appealing if somewhat threatening package.

"You talking to me?" She pointed a hand at herself. An odd stab of excitement raced through her as they exchanged a searing glance.

"I don't see anyone else messing around with my horse, so I must be talking to you. Who are you?" he demanded.

Not one to be intimidated, even by a man twice her size, Raleigh drew herself up to her full five feet and knotted her hands into fists. "I'm Raleigh Travers. Who are you?"

The man took a determined step toward her, but Raleigh stood her ground. He reached over and clamped a large paw on her shoulder.

Incensed by his proprietary manner, Raleigh turned and drove her arm backward, jabbing her elbow straight into his lean, hard, abdominal muscles. The instant she let loose, it hit her—she'd just assaulted her potential boss!

Daniel McClintock blinked twice and expelled his breath as he absorbed the unexpected punch. He stared at her freckled, pixie face in amazement. The tiny twister packed one hell of a wallop.

"Oh, my gosh. I'm so sorry. Did I hurt you?"

"Honey," he drawled, "what do you think I'm made of? Marshmallows? Of course you didn't hurt me."

"That's good." She whipped off her sunglasses and clutched them nervously. "I didn't mean to elbow you like that. I just hate for people to grab me."

"Don't worry about it." He fanned his fingers over his gut, surprised by the tingle he felt growing there.

"Listen, can we start over?" She pocketed her sunglasses and extended a hand. "I'm Raleigh Travers."

"Daniel McClintock." Dan touched her petite but work-roughened palm. The sudden pinching sensation, as if a screw had been tightened in his chest, startled him. He gulped.

Trouble was written on her face for anyone to read— dark shadows circled her gray eyes and her lips were pressed tight with worry. She held her thin shoulders ironing-board stiff in a tough, defensive manner. What heavy burdens did she carry? Dan wondered.

"Take a picture, it'll last longer," she snapped.

"Huh?"

"Didn't anybody ever teach you it's not polite to stare?" She crossed her arms and raised a quizzical eyebrow.

"Oh. Was I staring?" His fingers curled over hers and held them captive. She was a bristly little thing.

"Yes." She telegraphed him a steady glare until, embarrassed, he dropped her hand. The woman unnerved him, plain and simple. His gaze drifted over her delicate features. He admired her long, burnished copper braid, her peachy complexion, her strawberry red lips. Alarmed by the undeniable tug of attraction churning inside him, Dan tilted his head and angled her a sideways glance.

"Well, then," he said. "What can I do for you, Ms. Travers?"

"I'm looking for a job."

"A job?" he repeated.

"I heard talk in town that you might need a farrier."

"That's true," he conceded. "I do need to have my horses shod, but you're not exactly what I had in mind."

"I'm strong. I may be small, but I'm wiry."

Wiry is right, Dan thought, and swallowed. He could attest to that. His gaze traveled to the hollow of her long, slender neck. The cotton material of her tank top stretched seductively across firm, high breasts. Faded jeans hugged her hips like a surgeon's glove. Did she really expect him to believe she shod horses for a living?

"I can do the work as well as any man," she bragged.

He needed an inexperienced farrier about as much as he needed three thumbs. Considering the pressing time constraints facing him, he had enough trouble keeping to his schedule without a testy woman underfoot.

"Let me prove myself. Let me shoe that Thorough-bred." She nodded at the gelding. "On the house. Give me a chance. What have you got to lose?"

The look in her eyes challenged him. Intrigued by the woman and her unexpected lure, Dan nodded. "No harm in giving you a tryout, I suppose."

He wanted to see her in action. She had guts, no doubt about it. Waltzing in here asking for a job while at the same time dishing out a healthy dose of attitude. He suspected she'd developed her feisty demeanor as a defense mechanism. It couldn't be easy, working as a female farrier.

"Thank you," she said simply.

Her smile affected him like an arrow shot from a crossbow straight into the center of an oak tree. He could almost hear the vibrating thud.

"So, let's put you to work."

"I'll go get my supplies," she said, dusting her hands together.

"Let me help," he offered.

"No, sir. I'm going to prove to you I can handle all aspects of this job and that includes hauling around my own equipment. I don't want it being said Raleigh Travers can't pull her own load."

Dan doubted if anyone could ever say such a thing about this fireball. He'd known her a mere five minutes and already formed the distinct impression she was one no-nonsense lady. Following her over to the aging truck, he watched her back pockets sway.

Hold on, Dan, my man, now's not the time to be falling in lust, he cautioned himself. As if there was a good time to get tangled up with women. More than once, a shapely behind had orchestrated his downfall.

Hoisting a shoe box full of tools, a leather apron, a tripod and a wooden frame from the bed of her pickup, Raleigh strained to grip the supplies in both arms. Dan had to force himself not to help her. She was an independent cuss and he wasn't about to offend her again. A single swift elbow to the gut was enough for one day.

They walked to the corral, and Dan held the gate open for her. He breathed in the sweet, dry aroma of hay, horseflesh, West Texas sand and Raleigh Travers.

"Here, fella." She spoke softly to the gelding. The horse pricked up his ears at the sound of her voice, and whinnied in answer. "I'm going to give you a new pair of shoes."

Placing the shoe box, tripod and frame on the ground, she tied the leather apron around her waist and at the back of each knee. Opening a box of nails, she stuck a handful to the magnet sewed into the back corner of her apron.

Pretty ingenious, Dan thought.

"Well, don't just stand there, hold the horse," she directed.

Horses weren't the only animals she knew how to handle. Dan leapt to do her bidding, quickly grabbing the gelding's bridle.

"His name is Matt Dillon," he told her.

"Oh? You a 'Gunsmoke' fan?"

"When I was a kid," he admitted. "I always wanted a horse named Matt Dillon. See that stray pup over there?" He nodded in the direction of a rangy yellow dog lounging in the shadow of a hay baler.

"Kinda sad-looking," Raleigh said, eyeing the dog, who sat up and scratched at his long floppy ear.

"That's why I adopted him. His name's Chester."

"He looks like a Chester," she agreed. "So where's Doc, Miss Kitty and Festus?"

"Haven't acquired them yet."

"How long you been living out here?" she asked, waving her hand to chase away a horsefly.

"Little less than a month. Buying this ranch was a fulfillment of my childhood dream. I've always been enamored of cowboys and the West. One day I realized I'd already wasted too many years riding a desk in downtown Dallas. So I took my life's savings and turned my dream into a reality."

"So, you're renovating this place into a dude ranch in order to relive your childhood?"

"Partly."

He wouldn't tell her the real reason this venture had to work. Tightly gripping the supple leather of Matt Dillon's bridle, Dan closed his eyes and envisioned the dream—a money-making dude ranch, catering to wealthy vacationers from the East. His place would be talked about from coast to coast, and written up in travel magazines. He'd prove to the old man that once and for all, Daniel J. McClintock could stand on his own two feet.

For six years he'd labored at a job he'd hated, saving his money and preparing for the day he could break free from the stranglehold his domineering father kept on the entire family. His older brothers, Jamie and Mike, were firmly entrenched in the business. They would never escape. But he'd done it, and he was determined to succeed. He found the thought of returning home a failure and listening to his father's "I told you so" intolerable.

Opening his eyes, he returned his attention to his attractive visitor and away from the uncomfortable truth of his rapidly shrinking budget.

Matt Dillon offered no protest as Raleigh lifted his foreleg and rested it on her tripod. Bracing her back, she locked her knees around the animal's hoof, then dug in her toolbox with one hand. She located her rasp and started removing the clenches from the old shoe.

Dan watched Raleigh work. He was struck once more by her girl-next-door good looks. It didn't fit. Her delicate feminine features and her tough, self-confident persona. A frank contrast he found unexpectedly sexy. The girl unsettled him, and he hated to be thrown off-balance.

"Does this take you long?" he asked.

"About forty-five minutes. Why? You giving me a speed test? If you knew anything about shoeing horses, you'd know that's a darn good time. And just because I'm fast doesn't mean I don't do a good job." Resentment skewered her features, and in that moment Dan knew that somewhere along the line men had made her doubt her own capabilities.

"I was only making conversation. Stop getting your nose out of joint over nothing." Dan held the bridle with one hand, using the other to push his cowboy hat back on his forehead.

"I apologize," she said contritely. "I get defensive about my work. Nobody believes I'm able. After you get ridiculed enough, you cop an attitude. Pa always warned me about my temper."

"You've got to admit you don't live up to most people's idea of a farrier. A blacksmith is suppose to be a big, burly fellow, not a pretty young girl."

"I know." She sighed. "Trying to buck convention in this one-horse town is like spitting into a tornado. It gets you nothing but a wet face."

"You from Clyde?" he asked.

"Born and raised. Sometimes it's a real pain, you know? Everybody thinks they have a right to tell you how to run your business."

"I can see you love horses."

"They're my greatest passion."

He heard pride reflected in her voice. Her easy self-assurance intoxicated him. She believed in herself with absolute certainty, even if nobody else did.

She removed Matt Dillon's old shoe and plunked it in the dirt. Rummaging in her box for a pair of nippers, she located the tool, then diligently groomed the gelding's hoof, cutting away at the excess growth like a podiatrist trimming toenails. An odd odor of burning beans filled the air.

Chester got up, loped over and began chewing on the discarded hoof clippings.

"Why is he eating that stuff?" asked Dan, wrinkling his nose in distaste.

Raleigh shrugged. "Dogs love hoof clippings, don't ask me why."

"Ugh."

Chester licked his chops and sniffed the ground, eagerly searching for more.

"How long you been doing this sort of work?" Dan aimed his dog a disgusted look. Chester wagged his tail and rubbed against Dan's leg.

"Ten years," Raleigh replied.

"Ten years? But you couldn't be more than nineteen or twenty years old." Dan nudged Chester away. The dog sighed and sat down at his feet.

"Thanks for the compliment, but I'll be twenty-four next month." Her hammer made a muted ping-ping sound as she tapped out a new aluminum shoe against the wooden frame.

"You've been shoeing horses since you were thirteen?"

"That's how the arithmetic adds up."

"Where'd you learn?"

"My pa taught me."

"How come?"

"What do you mean?" She raised her head.

"Why does a man teach his petite, teenage daughter to shoe horses? It's dangerous work. You could get kicked, even killed." The thought of Raleigh getting injured disturbed him more than he cared to admit. One misplaced hoof and she'd crumple like tissue paper.

"You're no different from the rest." She snorted.

"Why? What did I say?"

"You don't think I can handle myself, do you?"

"Yes, I do. I just can't figure out why you'd want to. It's hard, dirty work. Look, you're covered in horsehair."

Stopping, she brushed hair from her clothing and glared at him. "I happen to be very good at my work and I enjoy it. Satisfied?"

"Okay, okay, forget I asked."

"Fine. May I finish?"

"By all means."

Moving her equipment to the other side of the horse, Raleigh started working on Matt Dillon's left foreleg. A few minutes passed. Dan tried not to be obvious, but he couldn't keep from studying her rounded bottom and admiring how fine she looked in a tight pair of jeans.

"You're staring at my rear end when I bend over, aren't you?" she accused.

"Yes," he confessed.

Her head bounced up. "Well, stop it. Just because I'm in a compromising position doesn't give you a license to ogle me."

"But the view is so appealing," he teased.

She frowned at him, her face shiny with anger. What would it take to make this girl smile? Dan wondered. Was she always so serious? Did she ever laugh or have a good time? Momentarily, Dan diverted his eyes, but the minute

Raleigh returned to her work, he allowed his gaze to stray back to her compact form.

Observing her was an enjoyable experience. She moved with graceful, conservative motions, as if reluctant to waste any energy. Not an ounce of fat clung to her hard, lean muscles.

"Such a good boy," Raleigh cooed to the Thorough-bred, and for one startled second, Dan thought she'd spoken to him.

"You talking to me or the horse?" he drawled.

"I seriously doubt you have ever been a good boy," she replied tartly.

At a loss for a snappy comeback, Dan stroked Matt Dillon between the ears, relaxing his hold on the bridle. The gelding took a step backward and flicked his tail, almost swatting Raleigh's cheek.

"Hey!" she groused. "You're suppose to be holding him still."

"Sorry," Dan mumbled, and tightened his grip. He felt like a chastised schoolboy. Why was he letting her get to him?

"Two down, two to go," she announced after completing work on the second shoe.

Good. He didn't think he could stand much more of this.

"Need to take a break?" she asked.

"Nope."

He blew out his breath through clenched teeth. What *was* this bizarre tug of sexual desire seeping throughout his entire system? He couldn't remember the last time a woman had stirred him this way without even trying. It had to be pure animal attraction. Raw chemistry and nothing more. He must control his hormones. The last thing he needed was in-depth involvement with some

small-town tomboy while he struggled to make his dreams
a reality.

"Come here," she said, stretching catlike. Dan jumped,
and feared he might swallow his tongue.

"Huh?"

"Before I finish, I want you to tell me what you think of
my handiwork."

He almost slid out of his skin hustling to her side. She
leaned over and lifted the gelding's foreleg for him to survey.

His arm brushed lightly against hers. A fast, hot heat
accelerated his pulse rate. She smelled wonderfully of
lemons, sunshine and horses. Blinking, Dan stared down
at the neat row of nails embedded in Matt Dillon's hoof.

"Well?"

"Looks good." Dan nodded. He didn't know much
about the art of shoeing horses and he hated to appear ig-
norant.

The sound of an approaching vehicle drew their attention to the driveway. A battle-scarred work truck chugged
to a stop and a bowlegged, middle-aged man got out.

"Pete?" Raleigh asked.

"Raleigh? Little Raleigh Travers?" Pete Grissom, Dan's
only ranch hand, dropped the sack he carried and opened
his arms wide.

Raleigh tossed her tool aside and launched herself into
the older man's embrace. Dan found himself curiously
jealous. He wanted to wrap *his* arms around the irrepres-
sible redhead. Immediately he dispelled the thought from
his mind. He couldn't afford the distraction. All his time
and effort had to be focused on achieving his goals.

"I take it, you two know each other," Dan said.

"You bet we do." Pete winked. "Raleigh is my god-
daughter and the best horseshoer in Callaghan County."

"It's wonderful to see you, Pete." She beamed, and the sight took Dan's breath away. He longed to be responsible for making her smile.

"You, too, sugar babe." Pete affectionately pounded her back.

"How long you been working here?" she asked.

"Close to three weeks."

"Well, this is fantastic. I'm going to be working here, too."

She was? Dan pulled a sour face. How to break the bad news? He just couldn't afford to hire her. At least, not right now.

"I do have the job, don't I, Mr. McClintock?" Untangling herself from Pete's embrace, Raleigh turned to face Dan.

Dan hesitated.

"I'm tough. I can shoe as many as eight horses a day. Want me to shoe some more when I get done with Matt Dillon?" A note of desperation had crept into her voice.

"Well..." Dan stalled, trying to think of a gentle way to refuse her.

"You're not going to give me the job, are you?" she accused.

"I didn't say that."

"You didn't say yes."

"Raleigh..."

"It's because I elbowed you in the gut, isn't it?" Her shoulders slumped in defeat.

"No. Oh, no," Dan denied.

"I need the work, Mr. McClintock. I need it real bad. I've got a little brother to support and I don't want to be a waitress or a secretary. I'm an outdoors girl. I love shoeing horses. Please. I know I've got a sharp tongue, but I promise to curb it. Please." She whispered the last word.

Oh, Lord, she'd cast him in the role of villain. But how could he possibly hire her? He was on an extremely tight budget with every cent accounted for, and he hadn't planned on employing a farrier until after the dude ranch opened.

Shaking his head, Dan took a deep breath. "I'm sorry, Miss Travers, much as I'd like to, I simply can't hire you."

Chapter Two

Anger exploded inside her. Not again!

An abrupt burst of adrenaline caused her hands to tremble and her voice to quiver.

"Oh, that's rich ... rich," she cried, her tone shrill and nonsensical. Pacing a circle in the dirt, Raleigh flapped her arms like a giant bird, flailing at Dan and knocking over her tripod in the process. Matt Dillon jumped, flicked his ears and snorted.

Rejected again.

She wanted to scream her frustration. She wanted to break something. She wanted to slap that apologetic grin off Daniel McClintock's face. Instead she clenched her fists and hitched in a jagged breath. She knew she was a good farrier, she knew it! So why couldn't she get a job? Simple. Because she was a woman.

"What are you smiling about?" she snapped at Dan.

"You look pretty comical."

Narrowing her eyes, she shook a finger under Dan's nose. "It's because I'm a woman, isn't it? Admit the truth, McClintock."

"No." His lips twitched as he fought laughter.

"You refuse to give me the job just because I'm a female, isn't that right?"

"Raleigh..." Pete Grissom interjected, attempting to mediate.

"It's all right, Pete. I'm used to being discriminated against."

"It has nothing to do with your sex," Dan said, drawling the last word, his dark eyes glistening with suppressed mirth and something strangely akin to desire.

"Liar."

Dan rolled his eyes.

"Okay, then, what is the reason? You think I'm too small to handle the job, don't you?"

"No."

"You claimed I did good work. If I think I'm physically capable, why can't you trust my judgment?" Raleigh knew she should rein in her maverick temper, but she'd finally had all she could take. For six months she'd been banging her head against closed doors, desperately searching for employment. Unfortunately for Dan, he was the one to suffer the brunt of her frustration.

"The reason I can't hire you has nothing to do with your size."

She stopped pacing and stared at him. Embarrassment replaced anger. Once again she'd gone off half-cocked. Hanging her head, Raleigh studied her dusty boots.

"Well," she said, "what is it, then? What is your excuse? Why *won't* you give me a chance?"

Dan shrugged, a sheepish expression on his face. "I can't afford it."

"What? You're creating a dude ranch and you don't have enough money to get your horses shod? You expect me to buy that line of bull?"

"Honest truth." Dan raised his hand in a Scout's honor gesture. "Every penny I own is invested in this venture. I won't be able to have the horses shod until I have some capital rolling in from the ranch." He spoke calmly, unaffected by her whirlwind temperament. "Pete's not even getting paid until I turn a profit."

"He's right, Raleigh." Pete nodded. "I agreed to work for room and board. Not having any pocket change keeps me out of trouble, plus Danny runs my legs off so I don't have time to spend money, anyway."

"See." Dan smiled angelically. "I'm not the heartless chauvinist you mistook me for." The sight of his upturned lips stirred vulnerable emotions inside her, emotions she hadn't experienced in a very long time.

"I owe you an apology," Raleigh said contritely, disturbed by her response to this man. "I overreacted."

"Forget it. I understand."

He really was a nice guy, she realized. His dark eyes crinkled at the edges when he gazed at her. They were the eyes of a dreamer, soft, bright and shining with a faraway light. For the first time since her arrival she noticed his well-shaped mouth, sensual and tempting. She was of a practical nature herself and found the hint of romance in him appealing.

"I'm truly sorry I can't hire you." He reached out, stroked her jaw with his thumb, then quickly dropped his hand. The intimate contact dazed her senses and she took a step backward. Her imagination instantly conjured up a vivid picture of Daniel McClintock planting a searing kiss on her lips. She shivered despite the broiling heat.

Feeling disoriented, Raleigh ducked her head and toyed with her braid. Probably the hot, West Texas sun had permanently baked her brains. This was not the time or the place for erotic thoughts.

"I better finish shoeing Matt Dillon," she said, clearing her throat. "After all, I did promise you one on the house."

"Don't worry about it." He kept looking at her as if she were a delectable confection.

"I'm a woman of my word and if I say I'll do something, then I do it. Besides, poor old Matt Dillon can't go around half-shod, now can he?"

"All right," Dan agreed. "Because I respect your integrity."

"Speaking of work, I got a heap of it waiting for me, too. Good to see you again, Raleigh," Pete said, returning to the driveway to retrieve his forgotten package.

Collecting her supplies, Raleigh righted the tripod and resumed her stance next to the gelding Thoroughbred, while Dan settled in to hold the bridle once more.

Disconcerted by the swirling emotions she experienced when she thought about Daniel McClintock, Raleigh forced herself to concentrate on the job at hand. She must squelch these feelings. Now. But try as she might, a curious ache blossomed deep inside her. The man's proximity had a devastating effect. Resolutely, she denied the sensations she couldn't quite identify.

Silence descended. Not even a locust buzzed. Only the soft in and out of breathing and the droning of lazy flies could be heard. It seemed aeons passed before she finished shoeing the Thoroughbred.

"All done," she announced, her voice echoing oddly in her own ears. Untying the bandanna from around her head, she mopped her heat-dampened face.

"Would you like some ice water?" Dan asked, releasing his hold on Matt Dillon.

"Sounds terrific."

She watched him disappear into the farmhouse, still trying to decipher the feelings he aroused. A few minutes later he returned, carrying a tall glass of water.

Their hands touched briefly when she took the glass from him and the contact resulted in another roller coaster ride. Their gazes locked. Her stomach lurched; her heart scaled her throat.

"Thanks," she mumbled, and downed the whole glass.

"More?" he asked.

She shook her head.

Neither spoke.

Dust motes danced between them on a shaft of afternoon sunlight, bathing the corral in a hazy halo. Heat waves shimmered like living things. The silver buckle on Dan's belt glinted brightly. Matt Dillon nickered. Suddenly the aging horse ranch was transformed into a mystical, magical place. Mesmerized, Raleigh couldn't turn away. She felt like a firefly in a jelly jar—captured.

"Raleigh."

He breathed her name on a sigh and she met his stare. Jolted, she realized a romantic relationship with this man would be like riding a bucking bronco—wild, unpredictable, with no hope of getting off unscathed. His aura of dreaminess served only to make him more dangerous by tricking her with an illusion of safety. She knew about dreamers, failure, and lost love.

"That's it, then," she said, dropping her gaze in an attempt to break the spell he'd woven.

"I promise, when the dude ranch opens, I'll give you a call," Dan said.

"Don't worry about it."

"I mean to hire you soon as I can."

Yeah, big deal. She needed a job today.

"You're a good farrier, don't let anyone tell you otherwise."

"Thanks."

Anxious to leave, to be on another planet, she pushed Dan aside and grabbed for her equipment. "Got to get a move on, you know," she chattered. "Places to be, people to see."

"Let me help you with those supplies."

This time she didn't balk when he picked up the wooden frame and shoe box. Her head swam and she couldn't think clearly. More than anything, she wanted to put distance between herself and Daniel McClintock.

They loaded her gear into the pickup and Raleigh hopped inside. "'Bye," she said, gunning the engine and throwing the old truck into a head-jerking reverse. She didn't feel secure until she'd traveled several miles down the road and her raging heartbeat had slowed to a normal pace. Perhaps it was a good thing she hadn't gotten the job. Battling the long-buried emotions Daniel McClintock evoked in her made it far safer to remain unemployed.

"You shouldn't have let her get away," Pete Grissom observed.

"Huh?" Dan snapped out of his engrossing reverie concerning a certain redheaded farrier.

"Raleigh." Pete cocked his head in the direction of her departing pickup.

"I couldn't pay her. What was I suppose to do? Stand behind her truck? Did you see the way she lit out of here? She'd have mowed me down like a field of Johnsongrass."

Pete stroked his grizzled jaw. "Could've offered her the same setup you're giving me. Free room and board, all expenses paid for six months, then ten percent of the yearly profits."

"If there are any profits," Dan said gloomily. Sometimes he felt he was kidding himself. Running a ranch was rapidly proving to be a much more daunting and expensive task than he'd first anticipated. Had his father been right, after all?

"Yep, Raleigh is one special gal," Pete mused. "And she knows horses. Me, I'm better at renovating buildings than I am at caring for livestock. She could look after the animals while you and I do the carpentry work. She's a right hard worker, too, plus she'd be an extra pair of hands. I don't mind telling you, we sure need some help if you aim to open this dude ranch by next spring."

"Give it up, Pete. I doubt she'd go for it."

"She might. Never can tell about that girl, and she's got her little brother to take care of, so she'll do whatever it takes to make ends meet."

"Tell me more about Raleigh." Dan leaned against the gate, propping his chin in his palms. He knew he should forget about her, but dadgummit, he found her intriguing and quite unlike any woman he'd ever met. "Why is she raising her brother alone? What happened to her parents?"

"Folks are dead. Her pa passed on in January. Kidney failure. Raleigh's a real private person and she hates for people to feel sorry for her."

"What makes her so touchy?" Dan found her hot-blooded nature fascinating. He came from a controlled, unemotional family, and he liked Raleigh's fighting spirit.

"Just her way, I guess."

"Does she have a boyfriend?"

"I don't like to gossip. Maybe you better ask her yourself."

"Come on, Pete. Throw me a bone."

Pete shrugged. "No. She ain't got a fella. Least not now. She don't go out much. Spends most of her free time with her brother, Caleb, or with horses."

"How come? She's cute and smart and talented. Why isn't she married?"

"She's got her reasons."

"Some man broke her heart?"

"Might say that," Pete reflected, nibbling on a piece of hay.

Raleigh in love with someone else? An unexpected lance of pure green jealousy poked through him. Who had hurt her so severely she wanted nothing more to do with men? Dan took off his cowboy hat and turned it around in his hands.

"What else?"

"It's not my place, boss. Talk to Raleigh."

Dan sighed. Maybe it was better if he let the whole thing drop. He had a goal to achieve and chasing after Raleigh Travers would only interfere with his plans.

"I wouldn't mind getting to know her better," Dan confessed. "But I'm not ready for anything long-term. This dude ranch is commitment enough for me."

"If that's true, I suggest you give her a wide berth." Pete spoke sharply. "She's suffered a lot in her short life and she deserves better than being your fling."

"You're absolutely right." Dan slapped Pete on the back. "I'm steering clear of her."

"That's good, 'cause if you hurt her, you'll have me to contend with."

Dan raised his palms. "Don't worry, Raleigh is strictly off-limits. But maybe, one day, I will find the right girl. I am a family man at heart."

"One thing at a time, boss. First, let's get this dude ranch in operation. After all, I have a stake in this investment, too."

Pete was right. His priorities lay in renovating the ranch. But that knowledge couldn't dispel the tantalizing memory of Raleigh Travers's unique smell or the destructive effects her tight little tush had had on his libido. He'd already learned one painful lesson about letting his heart rule his head. His track record wasn't exactly stellar. Nope. The best plan of action was to forget about Miss Raleigh Travers entirely.

Raleigh drove aimlessly.

Pushing her sunglasses up on her nose, she wrapped the end of her braid around one finger. She couldn't deny the volcanic undercurrent seething between her and Daniel McClintock, no matter how badly she might wish to do just that. They both recognized it. For one dizzy moment back there in the corral she'd been totally immobilized by his scrutiny, drawn like an unsuspecting insect into the spider's web.

She had wanted him to kiss her.

Groaning, she shook her head. The realization shocked her. Not since Jack had anyone made her feel so sensual, so attractive, so desirable. Shivering, she placed a hand to her forehead.

She felt panicky. Acknowledging the sensation, she immediately shied from it. Panic was a sure sign her emotions were involved. When Jack came to mind, a heavy suffocating breathlessness descended upon her as if someone were holding a pillow over her face. No. She would not think about either the past or Daniel McClintock. She would not allow herself to care about any man again.

The clock on the dashboard told her it was five-fifteen, but it perpetually ran ten minutes fast no matter how often she reset it. Caleb would be finished with his afternoon paper route and hungry for supper. At the thought of her younger brother, she sighed. How could she tell him she'd struck out one more time?

Pulling up outside the rented duplex she and fourteen-year-old Caleb had called home since their father's death, Raleigh cut the engine, swung to the ground, and sauntered up the front porch steps. She'd never grown accustomed to living in town. Raised on a farm, she missed the animals, the garden, the wide expanse of open land.

"Hey, sis." Caleb greeted her from the porch swing where he rocked slowly back and forth.

"How's it going?" she asked, reaching over to ruffle his hair. She knew the gesture drove him crazy, but she couldn't seem to help herself.

"Not good," he replied, solemnly smoothing down his hair and handing her a piece of paper.

"What's that?"

"Bad news."

Tentatively she unfolded the paper. An eviction notice for failure to pay rent.

"We've got to get out by the end of the month." Caleb tried to sound brave, but his quivering lip sold him out.

Scanning the letter, Raleigh sighed, crumpled the paper, and tossed it into Caleb's lap. "So what? We didn't like living here, anyway."

"But what are we going to do?" Her bother frowned.

"You let me worry about that."

"I can't help it. I worry, too." Caleb's steely blue eyes reminded her so much of Pa, Raleigh experienced a sad tug of longing for their father.

She held up her hands. "Listen, Caleb. Have I ever let you down before?"

"No."

"And I'm not about to start now."

His face brightened. "Did you get the horseshoeing job at the ranch?"

"Well, no."

Caleb gave her a hard look and sucked in a breath. "So, what *are* we going to do?"

"I'll take Fay up on her offer to work at the diner."

"Ah, sis, you'll hate waiting tables."

"It'll only be temporary, until a horseshoeing job opens up. You can do anything if you know it won't last long."

She told the lie for Caleb's sake. Once employed at the diner, it was unlikely she'd ever get the chance to work as a farrier. And taking the waitressing job wouldn't solve their immediate housing problems. The best wages she could hope for would total a hundred and fifty dollars a week, and the duplex cost three hundred a month. Even if she could talk their landlord into revoking the eviction notice, they couldn't afford to stay here.

Caleb's expression darkened.

"Come on," she said, patting his shoulder. "We've still got each other, don't we?"

Rocketing out of the porch swing, Caleb gave her a fierce hug. "You bet, sis."

They'd been through so much together. First, the loss of their mother, then Pa's death. If it weren't for Caleb, she'd have cracked up long ago. Hugging him right back, Raleigh marveled at how tall he'd sprouted over the summer.

A mere three months earlier they'd been the same height, now he topped her by a good four inches.

"I got paid from the newspaper today." He jingled the change in the pocket of his faded jeans. "How 'bout I treat us to a burger at the diner?"

She started to say no and tell him they needed to save every dime, but what did a few dollars matter when they owed hundreds?

"Come on," he wheedled. "I know you hate to cook. Besides, there's nothing in the house to eat and we'd have to go grocery shopping."

"Okay," she agreed. "My arm's been properly twisted."

"Great."

They piled into the truck and drove the few blocks to Fay's Diner. For Caleb's benefit, Raleigh tried to be cheerful, but her thoughts kept vacillating between the eviction notice and Daniel McClintock. Why couldn't she shake that man from her mind?

Ever since Jack, she'd been able to ignore men, easily laughing off their advances. But McClintock was different. Around him, she felt giddy and out of control.

"Hey, Raleigh, some of the guys from school are here. Do you mind if I go sit with them for a minute?" Caleb asked.

Raleigh blinked, realizing her thoughts had strayed. "Of course not."

"Gee, thanks." Scooping up his order, Caleb moved over to the table occupied by his friends.

Raleigh chewed her fish sandwich and sipped her cherry cola without tasting it. Finishing the meal, she waited while Caleb and his buddies talked, joked, and fed quarters to the jukebox.

Parenting a teenage boy required boundless energy and long-suffering patience, two qualities she often found herself in short supply of. Sometimes Raleigh questioned her abilities. Caleb needed a male role model, and that was one of the things she couldn't give him.

"Heck, I can't even provide a roof over his head," she mumbled under her breath, wadding up a piece of napkin and rolling it into a tight ball. Glumly, she stared at a clot of dried catsup clinging to the side of the napkin dispenser.

How would she make ends meet?

While a loud rock tune blared on the jukebox, Raleigh took her checkbook from her purse and assessed the reality of the situation. After subtracting the amount for their weekly food bill, they had a grand total of forty-seven dollars and fifty cents.

"Hi there, kitten. Watcha up to?" Fay Walton settled herself into the seat across from Raleigh. Fay was closing in on fifty, but appeared ten years younger. She maintained a youthful figure, wore perfectly applied makeup, and carefully dyed any stray gray hairs.

"Hey, Fay."

Raleigh stashed her checkbook back in her purse and smiled wanly at the woman who used to date her father. At one time she and Caleb thought Fay might even become their stepmother, but it had never happened.

"Why the sad face?"

Raleigh shrugged.

"Got turned down for another job, huh?"

"You can read me like a book."

Fay reached across the table and patted her hand. "It'll be okay."

"We're being evicted from the duplex."

"Oh, sweetie, I'm sorry."

"We'll find somewhere else to live."

"Come and live with me. I don't have much room, but you can stay until you can find another place."

"Nah. I appreciate the offer, but we couldn't impose upon you like that."

"Well, then, if you won't stay with me, at least come work for me. I know you have your heart set on continuing your pa's farrier business, but you're welcome to work here anytime. Not to mention the fact I could use the help," Fay said.

"When can I start?" Raleigh asked.

Fay looked surprised. "Tomorrow, if you want."

"That'll be great, Fay. Thanks."

"You're more than welcome. Be here at six for the breakfast crowd." Fay squeezed Raleigh's shoulder. "I better get back to the grind. See you tomorrow morning."

"I don't know what I'd do without you, Fay."

"What you always do. Survive."

Watching her friend disappear through the swinging doors into the kitchen, Raleigh resolutely squared her shoulders. She might have to wait tables for a while, but she vowed that somehow she would find a way to pursue her farrier career—and get Daniel McClintock out of her thoughts.

Chapter Three

Raleigh was taking an order from table number three when she glanced up and saw him.

Daniel McClintock parked his shiny, blue, three-quarter-ton pickup in the parking lot of the First National Bank of Clyde, and ambled across the street, heading straight for Fay's Diner.

She froze.

"Miss? Did you hear me? I said, we're ready to order now."

Panic, swift and hard, launched through her like a ballistic missile. She stared at the elderly couple seated at the pink vinyl booth in front of her. They gazed at her curiously.

"Excuse me..." She choked out the words. Zooming across the room, Raleigh snagged the other waitress's elbow as the bell over the door tinkled merrily and Dan strutted inside.

"Annie. Annie," she said in a rushed whisper. "You've got to do me a favor." Dan spied Raleigh and slanted her a sideways glance. He winked and she felt her knees turn to syrup. Simply looking at the man caused droplets of perspiration to collect between her breasts.

"What is it?" Annie frowned, clutching a pot of coffee in the hand Raleigh clung to.

The elderly couple shifted in their seats, nosily craning their necks to see what was going on. The old man raised a hand. "Waitress."

"Oh, shoot," Raleigh muttered.

Dan settled into the booth next to table number three. Her area.

"Switch sections with me," she pleaded with Annie.

"What? Why? That old geezer's signaling for you."

"You've got to switch with me, Annie." She spoke in a desperate whisper. Raleigh couldn't tolerate the idea of facing Dan again. "See that guy over there? The one in the black cowboy hat?" As she spoke, Dan removed his hat and set it on the seat beside him.

"Yeah." Annie grinned. "He's real cute."

"Well, I don't want to wait on him. Please switch sections and I'll give you the tips from both areas. Come on, say yes." Raleigh peeked over her shoulder. Her eyes met Dan's and for one brief second she felt as if she were tumbling backward into a bottomless well.

"Are you crazy, girl?" Annie perused Dan and her light brown eyes widened in surprise. "Why on earth wouldn't you want to wait on a hunk like that? He can eat crackers in my bed anytime. Sure, I'll switch sections with you. Take this pot of coffee to table ten and you leave that cowpoke to Annie." The older woman thrust out her ample chest, her breasts straining at the buttons of her bubble-gum pink uniform.

"Thanks, Annie. I appreciate this."

"Don't mention it, honey. Just get a move on. You think it's busy now, wait until the cattle auction lets out at two."

Keeping her head down to avoid any additional chance of catching Dan's eye, she scurried away, trying hard to concentrate on her duties despite the noisy clamor of clinking dishes, high-spirited laughter and the steady roaring of her pulse whooshing in her ears.

She poured coffee for table ten, then hurried to retrieve an order as the cook rang the bell for pickup.

It was her third day on the job and although she'd been performing well, she could tell she wasn't cut out for this kind of work. Her temper flared easily when someone criticized the food. She resented casual flirtations from male customers. She disliked the greasy smell clinging to her clothes and she positively hated the pink uniforms. And now, to make matters worse, Daniel McClintock had appeared to plague her very existence.

Raleigh took another order and turned to deliver it to the kitchen, but found Annie blocking her way.

"He specifically asked for you," Annie said.

"Tell him I'm unavailable," Raleigh groused.

"I don't know what you've got, honey, but it's you he's after. Might as well get over there and talk to him before he raises a stink."

Raleigh groaned. Okay. Fine. She could handle this. He was only a man, after all. No big deal. Right?

"I'll take care of him," she told Annie through clenched teeth.

"Wish it was me he was interested in. You should have your head examined. He's gorgeous." Annie raised her hand. "I took care of the elderly couple, so go ahead and scope out the cowboy."

"Thanks," Raleigh mumbled, feeling guilty for getting angry with Annie. It wasn't her fault Daniel McClintock was sitting there with a good-for-nothing grin on his smug face.

She forced herself to go over to his booth. Gripping her pencil and notepad tightly, she coerced a smile. "What'll you have?"

"I could say something that would make your back get even stiffer, but I'll refrain. I want to prove I can control myself." A smirk curled the corners of Dan's full lips. Without meaning to, Raleigh found herself wondering what it would feel like to have his mouth on hers, hungry, searching, demanding.

Unnerved, she peered out the plate-glass window at the empty street before her. She couldn't bring herself to look at him; she feared being ensnared by his magnetic stare. If she wasn't careful, she could care for this man, and that thought scared her like a tightrope walker crossing the Grand Canyon without a net.

"Raleigh."

Focusing on her notepad, she repeated the question. "What'll you have?"

"Some common courtesy might be nice."

"Sorry," she said abruptly. "You came to the wrong place for that."

"Testy, aren't we?"

"Listen, I'm pretty busy, could you order, please?"

"Okay." He closed his menu. "Cheeseburger and a cup of coffee."

She scribbled on the pad and spun away. But before she could escape, Dan grabbed the tail of her apron and tugged her into the curve of his strong, muscular arm. His hand molded around her hip. The feel of his skin against her polyester uniform sparked an inexplicable blaze inside her groin.

"Let me go," she stormed, stamping her feet for emphasis. Color burned her cheeks. Not one to sidestep a challenge, Raleigh sucked in a breath, fortifying herself for a fight. She hated how vulnerable McClintock made her feel.

As if sensing her growing agitation, Dan slowly released her, a pensive expression crossing his angular face.

Relieved to be free from his embrace, she raced away, only to be waylaid from behind the counter by Annie. "So, what's the scoop?" the waitress asked.

"Nothing."

"Ha! You're holding out on me. I saw the way he grabbed you."

"Waitress," someone called, and Raleigh was saved from replying as she bustled to their table.

Yet even as she took another order, her mind was on Daniel McClintock. Why couldn't he just leave her alone? The man made her feel restless and unsure of herself. She'd decided a long time ago to forget about men, and it was a good, rational choice. A decision based on common sense and one designed to protect her heart. Falling in love was too painful, especially when love disappeared. Besides, she had Caleb to think about. She couldn't expect any man to take on a ready-made family. It was asking too much.

She was happy with things the way they were. Well, sort of. If she could get her farrier business off the ground, then she would be happy. But she didn't need some arrogant man to make her life complete. She could manage just fine on her own, thank you very much.

The cook rang the bell and Raleigh picked up Dan's order. Her hands trembled as she set the cheeseburger in front of him and tried for a quick escape.

"Got any catsup?" he asked.

She snatched a bottle from an empty table and plunked it down. "Anything else?"

"May I ask you a question?"

"If you must." She sighed and settled her hands on her hips.

"How come you're working here?"

"I decided to go slumming and see how the poor and wretched live," she snapped sarcastically.

"You're too good of a farrier to be wasting your talents hustling tips."

"Thank you for your sage opinion, Mr. McClintock." She narrowed her eyes. "But seeing as how you couldn't afford to hire me, I took the only job I could find. By the way, how did you know I was working here?"

"Stopped by your house this morning. Your brother told me."

"What were you doing at my house?" He'd actually come looking for her? Excitement coursed through her at the thought.

"I came to offer you a job."

"Oh? And where did you get the money since Monday? Rob a bank?"

He laughed. The deep, rich sound thrilled her to her toes and she didn't know why. "No. I can't promise you money. At least, not until the dude ranch is open to the public."

"Such a flattering proposition," she said snidely, trying in vain to camouflage her attraction to him. "What do I tell them at the grocery store when they want hard, cold cash in exchange for a beef cutlet?"

"Tell them to put it on my account."

"I can see this job has limitless opportunities," she wisecracked.

"Actually, it does."

"Yeah? How's that?"

"Pete suggested it."

"Suggested what?" She couldn't deny he'd piqued her interest.

"Inviting you and your brother to live in the log cabin. Pete and I stay in the big house, so you'd have complete privacy. Room and board, all expenses paid, plus ten percent of the yearly profits."

She opened her mouth to refuse his offer, but instead she hesitated.

"Best deal you're likely to find in these parts."

It *would* solve their housing problem and get her out of the diner. But did she dare risk working for Daniel McClintock? What if these unsettling feelings she had for him erupted into something she couldn't contain?

"Of course, the job entails more than just shoeing horses," Dan continued. "You'd be in charge of all the animals and keeping the stables in shape. Pete and I have more than we can deal with getting the house, grounds, and guest rooms renovated."

"Caleb could do mowing, painting, shoveling out the stalls . . . things like that," she mused.

He nodded. "Sounds good."

The idea appealed to her—living in the country again, being near horses, working outdoors, her kind of life. The perfect solution to her problems, except she'd be totally dependent upon Daniel McClintock.

"Before I'd consider accepting your offer, you and I would have to come to an understanding."

"And that is?" He arched an eyebrow. It gave him the rakish appearance of a thoroughly bad boy.

"I want things kept on a strictly professional basis. Is that clear?"

"My sentiments exactly."

Somehow she didn't believe him. "No ulterior motives?"

"None."

"Then why are you extending me this proposal?"

"Because you're a good farrier and I'd like to help you get out of here." He waved his hand. "Plus, I'd benefit myself in the process."

"Oh, yeah?"

"Not a very trusting soul, are you?"

"Why should I be?"

The cook slapped the bell twice and scowled in Raleigh's direction.

"Gotta go."

"Saved by the bell," Dan observed.

"Humph," she snorted, and rushed off.

Considering the dormant feelings Dan stirred in her, working for him would be sheer lunacy. *But wouldn't it be great to work as a farrier again?* a little voice in the back of her mind prodded. Once people realized what magnificent blacksmith talents she possessed, others would hire her, then she could afford to move away from Dan's ranch and build her own clientele.

When she passed by his table, Dan lifted a finger. "Check, please."

"Sure." Anything to get rid of him. Digging into her apron pocket, Raleigh laid his tab on the tabletop.

"Did I happen to mention that I'm desperate? Not too many folks will work for nothing." He reached out and wrapped his hand around her wrist. His body heat radiated a warm circle on her skin.

"I—I..." she stammered, thrown off-balance by the intensity of his simple touch. "I don't think that would be such a good idea."

"Try it for a week. What could it hurt?"

"Not interested," she replied, purposefully twisting from his grasp. His fingers left a ghostly imprint of thirsty longing branded on her wrist.

He pulled a wry face and cracked his knuckles. Had their brief contact affected him the way it had affected her?

"Think about your brother. He deserves a nice place to grow up. Pete told me about your housing problems."

"Pete Grissom talks too much, and you leave my brother out of this."

A lazy smile crept across his mouth. He'd found her weakness and he knew it. "You could use the company truck. That heap you're driving is a road hazard."

"I'm not listening to you." She gathered up his empty dishes.

"Come on, Raleigh. What's the big deal? You want the job. I can see it in your eyes, they sparkled when I mentioned horses."

"Sorry, I can't work for you."

"Be sensible. You've got a teenager to support. What would be best for Caleb?"

He attacked her again with the guilt trip. Free room and board, all expenses paid. What would it hurt to try the arrangement for a week, a month, even a year? No. She couldn't risk becoming involved with Daniel McClintock. She'd been through too much pain to ever let herself become so vulnerable again. If the steady thumping of her heart was any indication, falling for him wouldn't be such a hard thing to do.

"No," she repeated. "'Fraid not."

"You don't have to give me a definite answer today. Sleep on it."

"I don't have to. Working for you would be a complete disaster."

"How can you turn me down?" He clasped his hands to the left side of his chest in a dramatic gesture.

"Easy. I'm heartless," she quipped.

Dan slid out of the booth and stood. "Think it over, Raleigh. Discuss it with Caleb. You can call me tomorrow. Oh, and by the way, pink is decidedly not your color," he said smartly, plunking his cowboy hat on his head and strolling out the door.

"Awesome," Caleb said when she told him about Dan's offer.

They were in the cramped kitchen of the duplex, dining on fried hot dogs, baked beans and macaroni and cheese that Caleb had cooked. He stopped shoveling food into his mouth long enough to swallow.

"It's not as great as it sounds," Raleigh cautioned. "For one thing, we won't have any money of our own."

"Yeah, but we don't have any money now and soon we won't have a place to live, either."

"True," she conceded.

"If Mr. McClintock pays for all the food and stuff, then we wouldn't need money."

"You'd have to give up your paper route."

Caleb shrugged. "Who cares? We could see Pete every day, swim in the pool and play tennis."

"Who told you about the pool and the tennis courts?"

"Mr. McClintock did. This morning when he came by to talk to you."

Frowning, she pushed a forkful of beans around her plate. Obviously Dan had already charmed Caleb with promises of material things—things she couldn't provide.

"Do you like Mr. McClintock?"

Caleb nodded. "He's real cool. You know what else he's got?"

"No."

"Video games. Can you believe it? A grown-up with video games? And he doesn't even have any kids."

That sounded like Dan, all right. A big overgrown boy. Instinctively she knew he was a relentless dreamer, just like Jack had been. How could she stake her future on such a man? What if his ranch went bankrupt? She and Caleb would be caught in the middle. Victims once more of life's circumstances.

"There's another consideration. Do you realize this ranch is ten miles out of town and there aren't any kids around? You'll have a hard time seeing your friends."

"Already thought of that, and guess what? Mr. Mc-Clintock said I could invite my friends over anytime. He even said we could camp out on the ranch. Pretty radical, huh?"

Mr. McClintock said this. Mr. McClintock said that. Apparently in her absence Dan had waltzed in and taken over her brother. Raleigh pushed back from the table, got up, and scraped the remains of her supper into the trash can. At the sink, she stopped the drain, squirted in liquid soap and turned on the hot water.

"Sis?"

"Uh-huh?"

"What's wrong." Caleb came to stand behind her. "This is an answer to our prayers."

With strings attached, she thought, irritated.

"That's the catch, Caleb. It's too good to be true."

Her brother rinsed the dishes as she washed, stacking them neatly in the drainer to dry. Raleigh cast a sidelong look at him. She saw disappointment etched on his freckled face.

"Caleb, I want to do the right thing."

"Then quit the diner and let's move to the ranch."

"You don't realize what I'll be giving up."

"Oh, like the glamorous world of waiting tables," he quipped.

"Caleb Brent Travers, don't you dare get smart with me."

"Sorry," he mumbled.

"Listen, the main drawback in working for Daniel McClintock is that we would lose our independence. I would no longer be a free-lance farrier. We couldn't come and go as we pleased. He would have to pay for everything. We'd be living in *his* cabin on *his* land," Raleigh explained, attempting to clarify her position.

"I don't see the difference. Right now you're working for Fay, not shoeing horses," Caleb persisted. "We're living in Mr. Vine's duplex and he's telling us to get out."

The boy had a point. Raleigh sighed. How could she make him see the difference and the inherent danger involved? She must avoid an entanglement with Dan at all costs, for Caleb's sake as much as her own.

"It's just not that simple."

"Okay." Caleb stopped rinsing dishes and turned to face her. When had he gotten so tall? "What's your answer? How *do* we get out of this mess?"

She stared at her younger brother, who suddenly seemed to be growing up too fast. "I'll get another job. I can work two jobs. And we'll move to a cheaper place."

Caleb shook his head.

"Not a good idea?"

"You'll be exhausted all the time and grouchy. You know how you get when you have to do something you don't like. Besides, what place would be cheaper than this?" Caleb swept his arm expressively, indicating their meager surroundings.

Peeling yellowed wallpaper hung in patches. The aging linoleum was cracked and worn thin. Two burners on the stove didn't function. The water faucet dripped continuously, and the refrigerator was at least thirty years old.

Raleigh exhaled deeply. Caleb was absolutely right. Where could they find a place more affordable than this and still be able to tolerate it?

"Do you really want to move to McClintock's ranch?" she asked.

"Yes. I think it would be good for both of us."

"I suppose we could give it a try."

"All right, sis." Caleb slapped her a high five. "This is going to be great."

Or perfectly awful, she thought.

Twilight descended over the ranch in muted hues of deep pink, dark blue and vivid purple. A yellow half-moon hung low on the horizon. The tantalizing hint of peanuts wafted on the breeze from the peanut field next door. In the distance a horse whinnied as the joyful chorus of a hundred singing crickets split the silence. Drawing a breath, Dan inhaled deeply, savoring the richness of the moment.

He'd forgotten over the years how much owning a ranch meant to him. As a child it had been his constant dream. He and his two brothers, Jamie and Mike, had spent their summers on a dude ranch. Despite the fact that his father had constantly scoffed at his plans, Dan had vowed to one day possess his own ranch.

He smiled into the gathering darkness. Well, it had taken him twenty years, but his dream had come true, or at least, it almost had. By spring, finances willing, the ranch would be open to the public.

Gazing out over the pasture, a feeling of pride and contentment welled up inside him so strong he was forced to swallow back the lump of emotion rising in his throat. At age thirty-one, Daniel McClintock had finally found his place in life. He knew without a doubt he was meant for this.

Working hard the entire day, he and Pete had made tremendous progress repairing one of the downstairs bedrooms. Another day or two and the room would be finished. Dan appreciated the way physical labor made his muscles ache, the way it caused him to fall asleep the minute his head hit the pillow. No lying awake at night tossing and turning and pondering the folly of his daily decisions, as it had been when he'd been employed at his father's plastics company.

How had he managed to waste so much of his life, first in college and then at a career he'd neither wanted nor cared about? Why had it taken him so long to gather enough courage to buck his father? Briefly he thought of Jenny, and grimaced. No matter, the past was over and his future looked bright.

Dan sat down on the tailgate of his pickup and watched the sunlight die. Chester wandered up and jumped into the bed of the truck beside him. Dan reached over and scratched the dog's floppy ears.

Inside the house, Pete was cooking supper and the delicious aroma of chicken-fried steak permeated the air, mingling with the scent of peanuts and producing in Dan a powerful sense of home, a feeling of rightness to the world. And then he thought of Raleigh Travers.

Even now, merely thinking about her, a heaviness settled in his heart and his palms grew damp. Falling for her would spell nothing but trouble. Because she'd be living so close if she accepted his proposal, Dan knew he'd have to fight to keep his emotions on a tight leash. He pondered the wisdom of his decision in offering her a job. She was a good farrier and he needed reliable stable help. When Pete told him about her dismal financial circumstances, he'd felt compelled to hire her despite his own rigid budgetary allotments. But was it a smart thing to have done? The push-pull of his conflicting emotions produced a tugging sensation in his chest.

Regretfully he recalled another time he'd fallen in love inappropriately. Jenny Harris had been a long-legged brunette, with a head for figures and a hunger for money. He'd been completely duped by her winning smile and calculating heart.

Dan winced at the memory. Running a hand through his hair, he marveled at his youthful trust and optimism. Even though he'd dreamed of owning a dude ranch, he'd allowed Jenny to talk him into going to work for his father. She'd promised him instant happiness, a wonderful marriage and lots of children. Because he'd been so blindly in love, he'd done everything she'd asked. His parents had thought Jenny had hung the moon, and a career in the family plastics business was the ultimate prestige their son could achieve. His powerful father, who wasn't used to taking no for an answer, had shelled out the money and ordered him to get an M.B.A. Nobody had bothered to ask Dan what he'd wanted.

As the youngest child, his desire to please others usually overshadowed his own goals. The few times he had voiced an opinion concerning his future, his mother had smiled and called him her Dreamy Danny, while his father had snorted and told him to get a grip on reality.

So he'd gone to college and obtained his M.B.A. Following graduation, he'd started working at the plastics factory just like his two brothers before him.

He and Jenny had set a wedding date. But when it became apparent to her that Dan would never be more than a peon on his father's payroll, she'd left him standing at the altar one sweltering July Saturday afternoon to run off with a multimillionaire ski resort owner from Taos.

The memory still hurt.

But with Jenny's departure, his old hopes and desires had roused and he knew it was indeed his one chance to make his dreams come true. He'd kept his job at the plastics plant, saving every bit of his money until he'd amassed a respectable pile, purchased this bargain-basement ranch, and told his father goodbye. His dad's derisive laughter still rang in his ears.

Closing his eyes, Dan envisioned his goal again. People vying for exclusive reservations at McClintock's World Famous Dude Ranch. Children riding horses, swimming, playing tennis, just as he had as a boy. Guests coming and going all year round. His father proud of him at last. And, by his side, an adoring wife.

He thought of Raleigh again and shook his head.

No. Not now. Even if Raleigh Travers was very different from Jenny Harris, he could not allow himself to care about her. For the first time, he was truly independent from his father's control and, for a while, he wanted to enjoy that freedom.

Sliding off the tailgate, he dusted his palms on the seat of his pants. Chester whined and thumped his tail for attention.

"Maybe she won't take me up on my offer," Dan said to the mutt.

Chester gazed at him and continued to wag his oversize tail.

"Problem is, I really need her help."

Chapter Four

The alarm went off at 4:00 a.m. Raleigh jerked awake and slapped the annoying clock into silence. Yawning, she sat up.

She'd dreamed of Daniel McClintock.

The dream had been hot, erotic. Very erotic. Perspiration dampened her forehead, and she found her covers wadded in a knot at the foot of the bed. Her body felt like melted ice cream. Clearing her throat, she pressed a hand to her temples.

Last night, after she'd made her decision to go to work for Dan, she'd called Fay and told her she was resigning. As always, her old friend was supportive, urging her to do whatever she thought was right. That served only to make Raleigh feel guilty. She'd spent the better part of the night flopping restlessly in bed trying to second-guess herself.

When she finally did fall asleep, Daniel McClintock had had the audacity to invade her subconscious. It wasn't fair, she mused. Definitely dirty pool. How was she supposed to resist a dream? Somehow, with one long, searing glance, Dan had penetrated right to the heart of her sexuality—a sexuality she'd thought long-since dead. She couldn't deny her attraction to the man, yet how could she afford to admit it?

Raleigh considered herself a strong person, but Dan had robbed her willpower, rendering her a wishy-washy mess. Closing her eyes, she could see him—thick black hair, quizzical dark eyes, hard, muscular body, imposing height. She swallowed hard. Her stomach jumped like popcorn in the microwave, pin-pinging with a sultry inner heat.

Blowing out her breath through puffed cheeks, she slid from the bed and flicked on the light. Her bare toes curled against the coolness of the hardwood floor.

She rifled through her closet, located her blue jeans and shimmied into them. Donning a T-shirt, she then pulled on socks and boots and braided her hair. Quietly, so as not to awaken Caleb, she tiptoed into the kitchen and made a pot of coffee.

Except for a sprinkling of stars overhead, it was dark outside. Early-morning dew clung to her boots as she crossed the lawn. Night noises lingered—the distant call of a meadowlark, the constant cacophony of crickets. The air smelled fresh, clean, hopeful. All normal, comfortable smells and sounds at a time when she felt neither normal nor comfortable.

What would McClintock say when she arrived on his doorstep ready to go to work? What if he'd changed his mind about hiring her? She'd be up the proverbial creek, because she wasn't about to inconvenience Fay again.

Balancing her steaming cup of coffee in one hand, she opened the pickup door with the other and carefully climbed inside. The contrary vehicle spat and sputtered before agreeing to come to life. Raleigh sat hunched over the steering wheel, sipping her coffee and waiting for the ancient engine to warm.

While driving down the darkened road to Dan's ranch, her thoughts were irresistibly drawn back to her disturbing dream. She couldn't remember ever having a dream so stark, so sensual. What did it mean?

"It means nothing, Travers, absolutely nothing," she growled to herself.

She had to stop thinking about him like this. Period. So he was good-looking. Big deal. She knew the risks involved in caring about a man and she'd chosen to never gamble on those risks again. Whatever she might be fantasizing about in her dreams, she could not allow herself to act on it. She had to maintain a professional detachment or this arrangement would never work.

By the time she reached the ranch she'd almost convinced herself to turn around and hightail it back home. But she couldn't. She had Caleb to think about. They had to have a place to live, and she wasn't dumb enough to expect another offer like this one to come along again.

"A woman's gotta do what a woman's gotta do," she muttered.

The ranch lay in a low spot between two hills. A fine white mist covered the ground. The old pickup rambled across the pasture and into the driveway. In the quiet of the predawn, trucks, trailers and ranching equipment loomed out of the fog like motionless prehistoric creatures, creating a spooky effect.

Raleigh shivered. Although the temperature was comfortable now, she knew that by noon the thermometer would soar to the one-hundred-degree mark.

For a moment she sat in the truck staring at the ranch and gathering her courage. Her next act might be irrevocable.

"It's now or never," she declared, resting her empty coffee cup on the dashboard.

Her bootheels made sharp crunching sounds as she trod over the graveled driveway and up the stone steps to the house. Taking a deep breath to assuage her nervousness, she rapped loudly on the front door.

She hesitated a minute, then knocked once more.

No answer.

Pounding on the door a third time, she paced the porch, her arms folded across her chest. This was not a good idea. She should leave while she still had the chance.

"Coming, coming, keep your pants on," she heard Dan holler.

A moment later he flung open the door and glared at her.

His hair was in wild disarray. A tuft of dark hair on the side of his head stood straight up. He wore pajama bottoms and nothing else. Raleigh caught her breath at the tousled sight of him.

"Good grief," he exploded. "What time is it?"

"Quarter to five."

"What are you doing here this early?" he asked, his voice softening. He raked a hand through his hair, and Raleigh had a sudden vision of him lying naked in bed. Her stomach tightened at the image. "Want to come in? I'll go put on a pot of coffee."

"Okay." She stepped inside, her emotions warring with common sense.

He closed the door and she followed him inside, her gaze darting around the living room. He'd tastefully decorated the place in a Southwestern decor of mint green, peach and sand. A rock fireplace occupied one corner.

In the middle of the large room sat two tan leather sofas, ottomans and love seat sets. A painted cow skull adorned the west wall, along with several Remington paintings. No wonder he couldn't afford to hire a farrier, he'd blown his dough on ritzy furnishings.

"Have a seat," he invited, waving his hand.

"You've decorated this room rather expensively for a man on a budget," she commented.

Dan shrugged. "I dream big. Sometimes my vision exceeds my bank account. When the dude ranch opens, I intend on drawing clients who are accustomed to the very best. This is the only room we've completed. You should see the rest of the house. It's a total disaster."

Easing herself down on the edge of the sofa, she clasped her hands together.

"Sorry I snapped at you when I answered the door," he said. "I'm not human until I have my coffee and I had trouble falling asleep last night." As if to illustrate, Dan yawned and scratched his bare chest.

"Oh." Raleigh averted her eyes from the sight of his stupendous pecs. Was she as responsible for his sleeplessness as he had been for hers?

"Excuse me a second," he said, and disappeared into where she supposed the kitchen must be.

Nervously, she crossed her legs, then uncrossed them again. She shouldn't have come so early, she chastised herself. Because Dan owned stables, she assumed he would be up and about at this hour tending his stock. The sight of him bare chested and in his pajama bottoms, so recently pulled from his bed, caused her blood pressure to climb a notch or two.

"You take anything in your coffee?" he called out a few minutes later.

"Black, thanks."

"Me, too," he said. "We've got something in common." He reappeared, carrying two steaming mugs.

Handing her one, he sat down next to her and blew across his coffee to cool it.

"You know," he said, "I must say you were the last person I expected to find on my front porch."

"To tell the truth, I'm surprised to find myself sitting here."

"And why is that?" He leaned closer and smiled wickedly.

She stared into her cup, carefully avoiding the challenge reflected in his eyes. "I came to see if that job offer still stands."

"Yes, it does."

"I want to start work right away. We need to move into the cabin as soon as possible. I lose my house in three days."

He nodded.

From beneath her lowered lashes she cast him a sidelong glance. He sat with his knees wide apart, forearms resting on his thighs in a casual masculine posture. Raleigh watched as his large thumbs rhythmically caressed the smooth ceramic mug cradled in both of his hands.

She was acutely aware of his strong, powerful body. Helplessly her gaze strayed to his bare, muscled abdomen, her eyes drinking in the dark trail of curly black hair that disappeared into the waistband of his pajamas.

Unbidden images rose in her mind. Visions sharp and graphic—his callused palms skimming lightly over her bare skin, his hungry lips suckling her breasts, their writhing bodies pressed tightly together against crisp white sheets.

No way. Sharply she jerked her head to dispel such torturous thoughts.

"Welcome to McClintock's Dude Ranch, Raleigh. I'm glad to have you aboard." Dan set his mug on the coffee table and thrust out his hand. Raleigh slipped her palm into his and let the handshake linger too long, enjoying the feel of his skin on hers.

"Well." He dropped her hand and Raleigh felt a distinct sense of loss. His dark-eyed gaze kept her pinned to the spot. "Guess I better get dressed."

"Should I go work with the horses?" Raleigh pointed her thumb at the door.

"Absolutely. See you in a few."

She leapt off the sofa, almost stumbling in her haste. Relief washed over her. She had a job she could enjoy and a place to stay. Only one problem remained. If Daniel McClintock decided to turn on the charm, could she resist him? Watching the man climb the stairs, Raleigh realized she could possibly be in deep trouble.

Dan backed the rented van into the driveway and stopped in front of the log cabin. Raleigh stood on the porch, a mop in her hand and a green bandanna tied around her forehead.

She'd scrubbed the place from top to bottom until it shone. Narrowing her eyes, she watched Dan open the back of the moving van. While he worked unloading her meager belongings, Raleigh's gaze traversed the lean muscles bulging beneath his bare shoulder blades.

Biting her bottom lip, Raleigh wished he'd put his shirt back on. The sight of his naked torso drew her undivided attention and sent her core body temperature soaring.

"You'll have to tell me where to put everything," he said.

Prying her gaze from his distracting figure, she shaded her eyes with her hand and propped the mop against the side of the house. "I'm not quite sure yet."

The log cabin contained only a living room, kitchen, bath and two bedrooms. It was smaller than the duplex, but in much better shape, and exuded a cozy rustic environment that smelled deliciously of cedar. The perfect dwelling for her and Caleb.

Bracing his knees in a firm stance, Dan wrestled her sofa to the edge of the truck. Grunting, he stopped and rested his hands at the small of his back.

"Here," she said, moving to stand beside him. "Let me help."

"No way." Dan puffed. "This thing is heavy."

"It's a sleeper sofa," she explained. "Remember, I shoe horses for a living. I'm perfectly capable of assisting you."

"Raleigh, don't be ridiculous. Let's wait for Pete. He and Caleb will be here any minute. Why don't you carry one of those lightweight boxes instead?"

"McClintock." She glared and rested her hands on her hips. "We have got to get one thing straight."

"Oh?" He turned to face her, his cowboy hat pushed back on his head, fine beads of perspiration gleaming on his bronzed chest. Unable to stop herself, she wondered helplessly what it would taste like to run her tongue along that very chest.

"I can handle physical work. I'm not some china doll to be protected. If you don't allow me to do anything laborious, I'll be pretty useless around here, and that makes me question your motives in hiring me."

"I just don't want you to get hurt."

"I won't. I know how to lift and I'm not any more likely to get injured than you are." She raised her chin, defying him to contradict her.

Reaching up, Dan casually brushed a lock of errant hair from her cheek. Raleigh stiffened and stepped back at his touch. Liquid fingers of heat spread through her like warm candle wax.

"Okay," he said. "You win. Let's move the damn sofa."

Shooting him a triumphant grin, she helped him heave the sofa off the back of the van. They struggled together and finally dragged it into the small living room. Raleigh had trouble handling her end, but she would never have admitted it to Dan.

"Let's put it in front of the fireplace," she suggested. "It'll be nice to burrow beneath a quilt in front of a roaring fire during a winter storm."

"Hmm," Dan said. "Now that does create an image. I can almost smell a pot of beef stew bubbling on the stove."

"And the sound of wind blowing against the cold windowpanes." Raleigh grinned, her mind easily conjuring up the cozy domestic scene in spite of the hot, slick sweat clinging to her neck.

"Country-and-western music playing on the radio." Dan brushed a damp lock of hair off his forehead.

"Playing cards." She twisted the end of her braid around one hand.

"Popping popcorn."

"Drinking hot chocolate with marshmallows."

"Making love."

"Huh?" Raleigh's face blistered at his words. No doubt her complexion turned three shades of red. "What did you say?"

Dan rested one knee on the arm of the sofa and looped a thumb through his belt. The action tilted his hips at an appealing angle. He stared into her eyes, binding her to him with an invisible string.

"Making love," he repeated, pursing his lips and cocking an eyebrow. "Isn't that one of the things people do in front of a warm fire on a frosty winter night?"

"I wouldn't know about that," Raleigh said in a brittle tone.

"Oh, no? Why's that?"

"There's more work to do," she said, pivoting abruptly on her heel.

Dan turned and, moving quickly, headed her off at the door. Determined, Raleigh pushed past him, her head down. She crashed into his side, heard his sharp intake of breath.

"Raleigh?"

They were all alone here, she thought, stepping out onto the porch.

Dan put out a hand and his fingers wrapped around her soft, pliant flesh. He pulled her to his chest. Their intimate contact affected him viscerally. Peering into her fog gray eyes, he felt his whole body harden.

How she fascinated him, with her fiercely independent spirit and her bullheaded stubborn streak. She rebuffed assistance, wanting desperately to survive on her own. How he understood that desire! And how he wanted her— beneath him, above him, in his arms, in his bed.

He held her tight, not wanting to let go. As he looked down into her startled, heart-shaped face, he realized her spunky attitude masked some heavy emotional burdens. At that moment Dan knew he longed to be the man to erase those difficulties, to show her life didn't have to be hard and painful if you had someone to lean on.

He lowered his head. She offered no resistance. How beautiful she was with the blazing afternoon sun dappling patterns of light across the freckles dusting her small, pert nose.

In his arms she felt so tiny, so vulnerable. It amazed him that she could readily control large horses with only the tone of her voice and firm discipline.

His body responded to those sensual thoughts. Firecrackers of awareness ignited inside him, causing his jeans to tighten in response.

He could so easily envision them locked together in the throes of lovemaking, her head thrown back, her glorious red hair fanned long and free over his bare skin. Her sweet feminine scent assailing his trembling nostrils, invading his very being. Her generous squeals of pleasure filling his eager ears.

Her lips quivered. Dan moaned softly and bodily lifted her off her feet.

"Oh," Raleigh whispered, and then Dan was kissing her like she'd never been kissed before. He pressed his lips to hers, wild yet tame, strong yet tender. Only her sleeveless cotton tank top separated his bare flesh from hers.

She gulped, her mind whirling. A white hotness boiled within her until her whole body simmered with vibrating need.

Dan deepened the kiss. His mouth searched, growing more insistent, more demanding, destroying her will, eroding her control.

Her hands seemed to have a mind of their own as she found herself kneading his rock-hard biceps.

His tongue feathered along her lips. He crushed her in his embrace.

She inhaled his unique smell—the heady combination of horse, spice, sand and man.

A driving force connected them. A force as natural and primal as stormy weather. Urgently she drank in the taste of him.

He twisted her braid around one hand and gently pulled her head back as his tongue thrust deeper.

An unexpected sound startled Raleigh.

She jumped. Could it be Pete and Caleb? From her peripheral vision she saw Chester lope up on the porch beside them.

Shame burst inside her with the power of an implosion. What on earth was she doing? She'd sworn nothing like this would ever happen and here she'd succumbed to Dan's masterful touch on her very first day at the cabin.

"Let me go," she cried, twisting away from him.

Automatically, Dan released her. She slid to the floor, her bootheels skidding on the worn wooden porch. Furiously, she raked a hand across her ravaged mouth.

"How dare you," she accused, reluctant to admit her own appalling behavior.

"Raleigh...I—I'm sorry. I didn't mean for that to happen." His eyes pleaded with her, but she turned from him at the same time Pete and Caleb pulled into the driveway.

"What's up?" Pete asked, slamming the pickup door and glancing from Raleigh to Dan and back again. Raleigh knew her hair was mussed, her face flushed.

"Did we miss something?" Caleb quizzed.

"Nothing," she and Dan chorused in unison.

"Hey, don't bite our heads off." Pete shrugged.

Raleigh caught Caleb eyeing her thoughtfully. Oh, gosh, what kind of example was she setting for her kid brother? This could not continue.

"Come on," she barked, determined to pretend the kiss never occurred. "Let's get this truck unloaded." She ignored Dan, grabbed a box from the back of the van and shouldered past him.

Her heart thundered like a prizewinning filly accelerating on the last furlong. Her lips tingled and her stomach fluttered. How could she have let that kiss happen? She should have seen it coming, moved faster, demanded he stop sooner.

Considering the distressing effects of Daniel McClintock's lips, she was a fool to stay here. But what choice did she have? She had no job and no place to stay. Essentially she was trapped—isolated with a man who could steal her will with a single, mind-blowing kiss.

Dan let out his breath through gritted teeth, hissing like a tire going flat. Remorse, sticky and cloying, wrapped around his heart. Pushing his hands through his hair, he leaned against the front porch railing and sighed.

Why had he kissed her?

Closing his eyes, he recalled how he'd gotten caught up in the moment. She'd looked so tempting with a fresh sheen of perspiration glazing her peaches-and-cream complexion, the gentle wisps of copper-colored hair framing her face, that jaunty green bandanna tied around her head.

He fingered his lips and grimaced. There was no denying it, she wasn't a woman to be trifled with. Dan had to respect her. She was no shrinking violet, that Raleigh.

"Boss?" Pete shot him an inquiring glance.

"It was nothing." Dan stepped through the doorway carrying a cane-bottomed rocking chair, and looked over at his friend.

"You sure?"

"Don't worry."

"Please, don't hurt her," Pete warned.

"Me? Hurt her?" The idea was ludicrous. If anything, he would be the one to end up with a broken heart. "Wouldn't dream of it."

"I certainly hope not."

Dan couldn't have agreed with Pete more. He'd made a big mistake. Although kissing Raleigh was the stupidest thing he'd done in recent memory, it was also the most pleasurable. And that spelled disaster with a capital *D*.

Spurred into action, he removed a floor lamp from the van and took it in the house. He stopped short.

Raleigh stood in the middle of the room looking more beautiful than he'd ever seen her look. Her tank top emphasized her modest assets, while her tight blue jeans flattered her attractive derriere.

Aching desire drilled through his swollen groin. He had an urge to fling her over his shoulder, carry her off to a cave and make her his woman. Yet at the same time his knees threatened to buckle at her very nearness. Around Raleigh he felt part tongue-tied schoolboy, part primitive Neanderthal.

Wrenching his eyes from her distracting figure, Dan chided himself. He had to quit thinking about her in this way if they were going to be working and living in such close quarters. The last thing he needed was another disastrous romance. Jenny had burned him badly. No—from now on, Raleigh Travers was strictly off-limits.

"Put the lamp in the corner, Dan," she directed. The calmness reflected in her controlled voice surprised him. Hadn't his kiss affected her at all? "Next to the sofa."

The same damn sofa responsible for instigating the unfortunate kiss in the first place. If they hadn't moved the sofa together...well...he would never have spoken those provocative words, never pulled her to his chest and clamped his lips on hers. Dan groaned inwardly and cast a sideways glance at her. He tried to decipher her innermost thoughts, but came up empty.

"Anybody for ice tea?" Raleigh asked, leading the way into the kitchen. She opened the refrigerator and removed a pitcher brimming with freshly brewed tea. Caleb unpacked the glasses, lined them up on the counter like attentive soldiers, then filled them with crushed ice from the freezer.

Pete pulled up a chair and sat down at the lopsided table. One of its legs was too short and Dan made a mental note to repair it for her.

"Have a seat, McClintock," Raleigh said, shoving a cold glass of tea in his direction.

Dan took the glass and pressed it to his forehead to cool his lust-fevered brow. He pulled up a chair next to Pete, suddenly feeling uncomfortable and out of place. Why couldn't he put the kiss out of his mind like Raleigh seemed to have done? She appeared totally unaffected.

"This place is great, Mr. McClintock," Caleb said, oblivious to the mounting tension in the room. "I always wanted to live in a log cabin."

"Thank you, Caleb. I hope you and your sister will enjoy staying here."

Dan kept his eyes trained on Raleigh. When she was in the room, he couldn't concentrate on anything else. She leaned casually against the kitchen counter, a glass of tea in one hand, the other hand cocked sassily at her hip. She glared at him over the rim of her tea glass.

Their eyes met, clashed. They exchanged an unspoken challenge. She flicked her braid over her shoulder and a quicksilver lick of desire lashed through him like a whip. Dan shivered.

"Cold, Dan?" she quizzed, never dropping her gaze.

"No. In fact, it's quite hot in here, wouldn't you agree?"

"It sure is, Mr. McClintock. I'm sweating like a horse rode hard and put up wet." Caleb wiped moisture from his face for emphasis.

Me, too, Caleb. Me, too, Dan thought, and the resulting spark of arousal chasing through his abdomen had nothing to do with the external temperature in the room.

"Please, call me Dan," he said, clasping a hand to the boy's shoulder.

"Okay." Caleb grinned. "Dan."

"No," Raleigh said. "I don't think that's such a good idea. After all, Mr. McClintock is our boss." She set her empty glass in the sink and crossed her arms over her chest defensively.

"But you call him Dan," Caleb argued.

"He's gotcha there, Raleigh." Pete smiled.

"Well . . . well . . . I shouldn't call him Dan, either," she sputtered. Flustered, she waved her arms in a gesture of dismissal.

"I don't mind." Dan grinned. He met her stare again, but this time she was the first to look away.

"Fine. Whatever," Raleigh muttered. "I don't have time to sit around gabbing, I've got work to do. There's a truck that needs unloading and horses that need to be fed." With that announcement, she turned, flipped her sassy braid over her shoulder once more and stalked past Dan's chair.

A devilish impulse overtook him. He felt the sudden need to get a reaction out of her, to break her supreme control. Before he considered the consequences, Dan reached out and captured her elbow.

She sucked in her breath, her muscles tensing beneath his fingers.

"Outside, McClintock. Now," she barked, wrenching herself from his grasp and fleeing out the open front door.

Chapter Five

Raleigh squinted against the brazen sunlight, wondering where she'd misplaced her sunglasses. In spite of the demanding afternoon rays, it felt good to escape the cabin's confines and Daniel McClintock's devastating aura.

When Dan finally followed her outside, she was grateful to discover he'd slipped his shirt back on. His bare chest had confused her so, she'd been unable to think clearly.

"We've got to talk," she said. From the corner of her eye, she saw Pete and Caleb standing in the doorway. "Somewhere private."

"Let's walk over to the stables." Dan tilted his head.

Raleigh didn't wait for him. Frowning, she spun around, tucked her fingertips into her back pockets and marched toward the stables.

She slammed into the barn, kicking the door open with her foot and startling the horses in their stalls. The animals weaved and neighed their displeasure at being disturbed. Pacing the hay-strewn aisle, Raleigh folded her arms and struggled to control her escalating temper.

Dan entered the barn behind her, his palms raised in a defensive stance. "Before you go off like a geyser, I've got something to say."

She kept stalking back and forth, taking deep breaths and spearing him angry daggers with her eyes. Count to ten, Raleigh, she coached herself. She'd tried hard to ignore the kiss, to pretend it was an aberration, but when he'd grabbed her elbow in such a possessive manner, right there in front of Pete and Caleb, she'd had no choice but to set the record straight.

"Okay." She managed to choke out that single word.

He arched a surprised eyebrow. "I'm glad to see you're willing to give me a chance to explain myself."

"Uh." She wasn't giving him a chance. She was too darned mad to speak!

"I didn't plan what happened on the porch. It was not a calculated seduction."

She shot him a disbelieving look.

"I'm just as perplexed by this thing between us as you are."

"I don't know what you're talking about," she denied, reluctant to admit even the slightest attraction to him.

"Come on, Raleigh. You may not like it, and heaven knows I find it damned inconvenient, but there *is* some force drawing us together. That's no reason for you to overreact."

"I don't know what you're talking about," she declared, petulantly flipping her braid over her shoulder with an arrogant toss of her head.

"Liar," he accused.

"What did you call me?"

"Admit it. Admit you felt those same white-hot flames of passion I felt. I could taste it on your tongue."

"I felt nothing."

"You lie, darling, you lie."

"I am not your darling and this has to stop."

"Why?"

"Why? Why?" she sputtered.

"Yes," he said calmly. "Why?"

"Because you're my boss!" She ducked her head, willing her heart to stop beating so loudly.

"So?" A taunting smile curled the corners of his mouth.

"It's unprofessional. And besides, I don't want to be attracted to you."

"I think this chemistry is something neither of us can control."

"I am not attracted to you," she insisted. She drove her fist into her open palm for emphasis. What was happening to her? She had to take command of this situation.

"Are you going to tell me I don't make your pulse hammer?" he casually leaned against one of the stalls and brushed a wisp of hair from her forehead. Involuntarily she shuddered and quickly pulled away.

"I told you when I accepted this job that being your mistress was not part of the bargain."

"I'm not asking you to be my mistress."

She blinked. "Then what are you asking?"

"I'm asking you to live here and run my stables."

"Then why did you kiss me?"

"It was only a simple kiss, Raleigh. Don't read any more into it than that."

Only a kiss? If that was only a kiss, then what would his full-fledged lovemaking feel like? An all-out invasion of the senses?

"Are you in the habit of kissing strangers?"

"Just the pretty ones."

She knew he was teasing, but she wasn't about to be cajoled out of her anger. She must ignore these emotions he awoke in her, the feelings she'd buried along with Jack. She'd promised herself she'd never fall in love again, never expose her vulnerable inner self or place her fragile heart in such jeopardy.

Life continually robbed her of her loved ones, so if she never loved again, she would not have to experience the repeated pain of unbearable loss. Long ago, she'd come to grips with a lonely future, in fact, had embraced it. She didn't need Dan. Didn't need any man.

Raising her chin, Raleigh renewed her resolve. "I'm sorry, but I don't think I can continue to work here."

"Please reconsider. I need you and you need a place to stay."

She shook her head. "I can't allow you to kiss me whenever the mood strikes you. I have feelings, too, you know."

"I know," he whispered softly. Remorse glimmered in the depths of his dark eyes. "I was wrong."

"Darned straight, you were wrong."

"I don't want you to leave."

"There's only one way I can possibly stay."

"Which is?"

"You've got to promise to keep your distance from me."

"I can do that."

"Can you?"

Dan nodded. "I confess, things got out of hand, but I assure you it won't happen again. At least not until you want it."

"Don't hold your breath."

"So you'll stay?"

"I do need the job." She hesitated, her thoughts ajumble. "And I'm excited about doing farrier work again. So here's my conditions. The cabin, barn and stables are my territory. You keep to the big house. Caleb and I will see to our duties. If that's not good enough for you, then forget it."

"I can accept those terms."

"And you get out of line even one more time and Caleb and I are history. Got it?" She shook her index finger.

"Loud and clear."

From his stall in the corner, Matt Dillon whinnied as if in agreement.

"I mean it, McClintock."

"I have no doubts about that."

"So it's settled."

"Want to shake on it?" Dan asked, grinning.

"Don't push me," she warned.

Chester trotted into the barn, sidled up to Raleigh and sniffed at her pant leg.

"Look," Dan said. "You can't leave. Chester adores you."

"He does not. He's just hoping I'll shoe a horse so he can have the hoof clippings," she scoffed, edging the dog away from her with the toe of her boot.

"What happened to you, Raleigh? You're so cynical you won't even let yourself show affection for a dog."

"That's not true!" she exclaimed, disturbed by Dan's accurate assessment.

"Then why did you overreact to our kiss?"

Had she overreacted? Raleigh didn't think so.

"Raleigh?"

She heard his voice but she didn't respond.

"Raleigh," he repeated firmly.

"Go away," she said. "I don't have anything more to say to you."

"Would you look at me? Please?"

Straightening, she turned to face him.

"I don't know why you're so afraid to get close to me, but I promise to respect your wishes. You don't have to worry. I won't force myself on you. Will you stay? I need your expertise. You know far more about horses than either Pete or I."

She needed time to herself, to think, to ride. "Can I take one of the horses out?" she asked.

"Sure. Anytime. You're in charge of them, remember?"

"I'll take that chestnut," she said, inclining her head in the direction of a sassy, bright-eyed mare. "What's her name?"

"Little Bit of Sunshine."

Raleigh nodded her approval. "I like it."

"Pete calls her Sunny."

Striding over to the stall, Raleigh picked a bridle off the wall and placed it on the frisky mare. She led her out of the barn and into the exercise yard.

"Do you mean you're going riding right now?" Dan asked.

She could feel the intensity of his stare warming her back. "Yep. I think better astride a horse."

"Bareback?"

"It's the only way to fly."

Positioning a booted foot on the bottom rung of the gate, Raleigh boosted herself onto the horse's back. The mare whickered and tossed her mane, obviously eager to be set free.

"Would you mind opening the gate?" she asked Dan.

"Certainly. You are coming back, aren't you?"

"Hmm," she replied, wheeling the mare out onto the open prairie. The chestnut, happy at being given her head, kicked her hooves in the air and sprinted over the yellowed grass, dried tumbleweeds and prickly cacti.

"Go, Sunny, go," Raleigh urged, leaning forward against the mare's neck and savoring the feel of the wind rushing through her hair.

Casting a glance backward, she saw Dan standing in the distance, still watching her. Her heart hitched in her chest at the sight of him. Reluctant to dwell on the meaning of their encounter, she pushed those thoughts from her mind. She didn't want to think, wanted only to ride and ride and ride.

Orange tongues of sunlight streaked the sky. A crow cawed from a mesquite. Sunny's long, dark mane whipped at her face, but Raleigh didn't mind the tiny stings. She pressed closer, taking comfort from the animal the way she could never take comfort from people.

Raleigh sorely missed her own horse, a beautiful palomino named Lucky. Pa had bought the animal for her thirteenth birthday. She'd been forced to sell the old mare along with their mortgaged farm when Pa died. One more heartache in a relentless string. One more reason to keep her true feelings chained.

Despite herself, her thoughts drifted back to Daniel McClintock. The man confused her. He shouldn't have kissed her, but if she were honest, wouldn't she confess she'd allowed the kiss to happen, had even enjoyed it?

An uncertain misery simmered inside her. She believed herself to be very controlled when it came to men. After Jack, she'd had no choice. She couldn't afford to lose herself to poor judgment and runaway lust. Raleigh Travers was much too smart to get caught in such traps. She knew her own mind and her obligations to Caleb prevented her passion from taking precedence over common sense.

But it was true, Daniel McClintock had gotten to her. She felt ashamed. She hated her own weaknesses. Was she angry with Dan or her body's own treacherous betrayal?

The incessant heat eased as August melted into September and cottonwood trees shed their golden leaves. Bales of freshly harvested hay dotted the fields. The mass of sunflowers crowding the landscape wilted and died. School started again and with it, the appearance of a rumbling orange school bus at the end of the dirt road each morning and evening.

Dan sat at his desk, staring into space, lost in thought. It had been three weeks since Raleigh Travers and her younger brother had moved into his log cabin. Three weeks of fighting a growing, almost unquenchable fire burning inside him. Three weeks of denying his need for her.

Absentmindedly, he tapped his teeth with the end of a pencil and sighed. Try as he might, he could not reconcile the monthly expenses. The invoice for an enormous feed bill sat in front of him. Fidgeting, Dan got to his feet and went to stand at the window.

His gaze traveled to the corral where Raleigh worked taming a skittish mare. Watching her, he marveled at her natural talents with the sturdy animals. Admiration for her brought a smile to his lips.

In no time she had whipped his flagging stables into shape, shoeing all the horses, engaging them in daily workouts, doctoring their wounds, repairing the aging stalls. He was amazed at her rapid progress. No man could have made a better hand.

Sliding off the back of the mare, Raleigh tied the horse to the gate, then stretched sexily in the sun. He stifled a groan. Keeping his desire under wraps proved to be a much tougher task than he'd imagined when he'd made his promise to her. How he longed to hold her, kiss her, make love to her, slow, sweet and easy.

Tossing her braid over her shoulder, Raleigh looked up and caught him staring at her. Gulping, Dan stepped back from the window.

For three weeks he'd managed to maintain his distance, but every day it became harder and harder to ignore the magnetic pull. Observing her, but unable to touch her, produced a profound sense of melancholy deep in his soul. Sooner or later, something had to give.

When he realized she was coming up the walk toward the house, her fingertips tucked into her back pockets in that endearing gesture of hers, excitement surged through his veins like a strong tonic. Not once since she and Caleb had moved in had she been to the big house. What did this unexpected visit signify?

Holding his breath, Dan stood motionless, waiting for her knock. When the sound came, he jumped, then hurried to throw open the door.

"'Morning, Raleigh," he greeted her, hoping he appeared nonchalant. It wouldn't do for her to guess the depth of his feelings. If she had any idea what he'd just been imagining, she'd pack up and be off the ranch by nightfall.

"Can I talk to you for a minute?" Her steady, gray-eyed stare blistered a trail to his heart. She was different from any woman he'd ever known—so strong, so independent, so self-reliant. How had she gotten that way? The mystery of her exceptional personality intrigued him to no end.

"Sure, come on in." Standing aside, he held out his arm. Her boots echoed on the parquet tile as she stepped over the threshold.

"Can I get you something to drink?" he offered.

"Glass of water would be nice," she said, wiping her flushed face with a blue bandanna plucked from her pocket.

"Have a seat. I'll be right back."

When he returned to the den, he found her leaning over his desk studying the stack of bills.

"You're three thousand dollars in the hole," she commented frankly.

How had she figured that out in the short time he'd been in the kitchen? Dan scooped up the papers, clutching them in his hand. "It's not your worry."

"Oh, no?" She raised both eyebrows.

"Here's your water."

She took the glass from him, seated herself on the edge of his desk and took a sip. Helplessly, his gaze strayed to survey the attractive way her jeans creased across her compact lap.

"If the ranch goes bankrupt, Caleb and I will no longer have a place to stay, and remember, you promised me ten percent of the yearly profits. If there are no profits, I'm as broke as you. Now, I'd definitely say it's my problem, too."

Sinking down in his overstuffed chair, Dan set the bills back on the desk and templed his fingers. "Fair enough. I'll level with you. Yes, I'm experiencing a financial crunch I hadn't anticipated."

She swung her leg, eyeing him thoughtfully. "Want to know what I think?"

"Sure."

"You're going about this business all wrong."

"Oh, yeah?" So she thought she was a business expert, did she?

"Yep."

Dan cracked his knuckles. She was too darned distracting. He couldn't help but notice the way her tank top strained across her pert breasts and flattered her waspish waist. He wished she wouldn't wear those barely there shirts, but he knew it was simply a matter of comfort while she worked outside in the sweltering heat.

"Dan?" She leaned forward and snapped her fingers in his face. He caught a whiff of her fresh, natural scent and immediately thought of haystacks, sunshine and wild horseback rides across sandy fields.

"Huh?" He blinked.

"Did you hear me?"

"I'm sorry, what were you saying?" He shook his head to dispel the erotic fantasies his mind had conjured up. He had to stop thinking like this, no point in torturing himself.

"I said, you're going about this business all wrong."

"What do you mean?"

"You need to be more practical. I realize you've got this grand dream for the future, but the fact remains, you need money today."

"Go on." What would it hurt to listen to her suggestions? Dan picked up his pencil and tapped it restlessly against the desk.

"In fact, I came in to bring you a list of stable supplies you've got to purchase." She removed a folded piece of notepaper from her hip pocket and handed it to him. "First, you should utilize the horses now instead of waiting for the dude ranch to open. Make them earn their keep."

The paper was still warm from her body heat. It rested in his palm like melted butter. She had tight, controlled handwriting. The signature of a perfectionist. Dan swallowed back stark desire and glanced over the list, tapping his pencil faster, harder, against the desk.

"The total price will run you about a thousand dollars. But you'll have to have everything on the list if you intend on running a top-notch dude ranch."

"We *do* want McClintock's Dude Ranch to offer the very best."

"Then it'll cost you."

"I've discovered everything in life has a price," he said, drumming the pencil at a frantic pace.

She reached out and touched his hand. "Could you stop? That's driving me crazy."

The feel of her skin against his caused his throat to constrict. Soft sprouts of hair framed her face, tempting him to brush them away. Her full lips lay far too close. Grasping the pencil firmly in his hand, he heard the crack of wood as it snapped between his fingers.

"Your wish is my command," he croaked.

She slid off the edge of his desk, oblivious to her effect on him. "You know," she said, "I do have a few ideas for bringing in more money."

"Bounce 'em off me." Dan tossed the pencil pieces into the wastebasket, dusted his hands together and sat up straighter in his chair.

"We could get people to board their horses with us. I'm a trained farrier, so you can include my services along with the boarding fees, and Caleb can help with the grooming. I know of at least three people looking for a place to stable their horses."

Dan nodded. "We could advertise. Marketing, that's the key. Why don't you call those folks you know and offer our stable services for whatever fee you think they'll be willing to pay."

"You don't mind?"

"Good grief, why should I?"

Raleigh shrugged. "I didn't want to overstep my bounds."

"Hey, like you said, it's your worry, too."

"I thought of another way to bring in money this fall and winter," Raleigh continued, ticking off the options on her fingers.

"Spill it, Travers." Heck, how could the dude ranch fail with someone as bright and hardworking as Raleigh on his team?

"We'd have to get a few rooms ready fast," she mused.

"What? You've piqued my interest. Don't keep me in suspense."

"Hunters."

"Hunters," he repeated, the concept appealing to him. Why hadn't he thought of it?

"Sure. There's plenty of city men looking for a place to get away from it all—the job, the rat race, the wife and kids. What better place than here?"

"You think it would work?"

"Sure. Pete and I both know how to dress game. We could offer a 'you kill it, we clean it' proposition. It would be fairly cheap to have flyers printed up and we could take out ads in sports magazines and daily newspapers around the state. 'Course, we better hurry, hunting season opens soon."

"We could advertise in gun shops and on the local radio station," Dan suggested, getting into the swing of things.

"Now you're cooking." Raleigh grinned and Dan realized just how infrequently she smiled. The disarming sight delighted him all the way to his toes.

"We'd have to build some deer blinds. Two or three ought to do. If you and me and Pete got right on it, we could erect them in a few days."

Excitement bubbled up inside Dan. He'd certainly hired himself a ringer, smart and pretty, to boot.

"Any other suggestions?"

"I could give riding lessons to kids and saddle-train horses."

"Excellent ideas."

"You really think so?" She beamed.

"Honey, you're an answer to my prayers." Belatedly he realized he'd called her "honey." Cringing, he glanced sideways at her to see how she would react.

An enigmatic look crossed her face, but she said nothing.

"Anything else?" he asked.

"We could host a hayride, barbecue, barn dance. Have contests and games. Charge a flat fee for large groups like the high school or local churches. Believe me, there's not much for kids to do in this town. The community would support it. I know they would." Raleigh rubbed her palms together.

"What kind of money do you think these projects might net us?"

"Depends. Maybe fifteen hundred a month, but at least we'd have a steady income while we readied the dude ranch for opening in the spring."

"Travers," he said with heartfelt enthusiasm, "you're magnificent."

And she was. While he was a head-in-the-clouds dreamer, cooking up grand schemes, she was a nuts-and-bolts, hands-on pragmatist. Together they made a terrific pair. Two halves of a whole. He thought of his skeptical father and smiled. Success, after all, was the best revenge.

Euphoria dissipated his earlier pessimism. Without thinking, he pulled Raleigh into his arms and spun her around the room. He didn't realize his mistake until he felt her stiffen against him.

Looking down, he saw her gray eyes had clouded like a pewter mist. Once more, she'd erected that blamed wall around herself. A wall that confused and disturbed him. One minute she was laughing and carefree, the next, serious and distant. He promptly set her on the floor and stepped back.

"I'm sorry," he apologized. "I didn't mean to manhandle you like that."

"It's okay," she mumbled.

An awkward silence descended over them. "I better get back to work. I only came in to give you that list." She indicated the desk with a wave. He noticed her chest rose and fell in a sharp, rapid rhythm.

"Thanks for the ideas. I really appreciate your input."

She studied her boots. "Just protecting my own interests."

He wanted to tell her not to be afraid of him. To allow the attraction stirring between them to simply happen, yet he sensed she wasn't ready.

Considering his own track record when it came to romance, he should be the one drawing away, but somehow he couldn't let pain and loss stop him from pursuing something special. If she would only let him in, tell him her secrets. He longed to recapture the instant joy of the moment just past.

"Raleigh?"

"Yes?" She raised her head to face him.

"Thank you."

"You're welcome."

Then she was out the door, leaving Dan alone with his dangerous thoughts.

Raleigh, Pete and Dan spent the next two days building deer blinds. Personally, Raleigh despised hunting, but it was the fastest way to earn ready cash. And that was her ultimate goal—help Dan turn a profit as quickly as possible, collect her share of the earnings and clear out of here before she got any more involved than she already was.

Then she would have enough funds to start rebuilding her father's farrier business. Which was all she'd ever wanted in the first place.

They worked side by side for hours, stopping only for a sack lunch and occasional water breaks. To Raleigh's dismay, Dan had removed his shirt early on and she'd spent the better part of the afternoon trying to avoid staring at his superb form. Several times she caught herself studying his glistening torso and the seductive way his muscles moved in concert as he busily hammered the wooden structure. Forcibly, she returned her attention to her work, only to find her gaze straying back to his body a few minutes later.

They finished before sunset, all three stepping back to admire their handiwork.

"I think we should establish a seasonal schedule of events, what do you think?" she asked Dan, placing her hands to the small of her back and stretching out the kinks.

He didn't answer.

"Dan?"

"Huh?" He snapped to attention, that dreamy, faraway look in his eyes.

"Earth to McClintock. Come in McClintock."

"Sorry," he apologized. "My mind wandered."

"Well, herd it back to the present decade, okay?"

Pete chuckled. "Keeping Dan's head out of the clouds is an uphill battle."

"I prefer to think of it as brainstorming." Dan grinned. "Suppose we bought a chuckwagon. A lot of ranches are starting to have old-fashioned cattle drives. You know, like in that movie *City Slickers,*" Dan mused, stroking his chin.

"You don't have any cattle," Raleigh observed wryly.

"And if you think I'm cooking on a chuckwagon, you're sadly mistaken," Pete assured him.

Dan waved a hand. "I'm thinking about future projects. We'd hire a cook, of course. We're going to have to do that, anyway."

"I hate to be the voice of reality," Raleigh said. "But if we don't get something going soon, there won't be a future."

"Trust you to bring me down to earth," Dan said, and the look he gave her zinged hot flashes straight to her stomach.

"Yeah, at this rate I'll be living on the ranch all my life." She shook her head ruefully.

"Sounds like heaven to me," Dan teased.

"Well," she said, purposefully ignoring his last remark and the sudden acceleration of her pulse. "We're through here. How about we get started repairing the plumbing in the downstairs bathroom at the farmhouse?"

Dan consulted his watch. "It's almost four o'clock. I vote we forget the plumbing and call it a day. We've been at this since dawn."

"You sure? I wouldn't mind working for a couple more hours," Raleigh said.

"Well, actually..." Dan confessed, "I've got a surprise."

"Oh?" Pete and Raleigh looked at him expectantly.

Dan plucked his shirt from a nearby fence post and fished in the pocket for an envelope. "Guess what came in the mail today."

Raleigh shook her head.

"Reservations from a group of four hunters and a check for six hundred dollars. They saw the ad in the Abilene newspaper." He grinned big as Texas. "I was hoping somebody might feel up to a celebration."

"Sorry, boss, Friday night is my poker night," Pete said. "But you two go right ahead."

Dan wriggled his eyebrows at Raleigh. "What do you say?"

"I don't think so," she hedged.

"Dinner at a swanky restaurant in Abilene? Come on," he wheedled. "I want to do something special for you. You've been working so hard, you deserve a treat."

Raleigh hesitated. It would be nice to go out for once, but did she dare risk it, considering the way Daniel McClintock made her feel?

"What about Caleb?" Raleigh asked. "Can he come, too?"

"Isn't this the night he's supposed to sleep over at a friend's house?"

Shoot, she'd forgotten about that. "Yeah, it is," she reluctantly admitted. With Caleb away, she had no ready excuse to hide behind.

"So?" Dan waited. "You're not going to make me celebrate by myself, are you?"

Since the day she'd issued her ultimatum to him, Dan had managed to keep a respectful distance, not once stepping out of line or misbehaving. Maybe she could trust him, after all.

"I'll let you pick the restaurant," he cajoled.

"Go on, Raleigh," Pete encouraged. "You need to have a little fun."

"All work and no play..." Dan said.

"I've got laundry to do tonight," she evaded.

"I promise not to bite. But if you're too scared of being alone with me, I understand."

"Oh, all right," she acquiesced. She didn't want Dan to think she was afraid of him. "But only dinner."

"Perfect." Dan smiled. "I'll give you a ride back to the cabin so you can get changed, then I'll pick you up in an hour." He winked.

The conspiratorial action blasted a jolt of pleasure up from the bottom of her feet. The man possessed enough charisma to dissolve forged steel. Her heart did flip-flops as a shiver of apprehension shot through her.

By agreeing to have dinner with him, had she just committed a fatal error?

Chapter Six

What on earth was she going to wear?

Fresh from the shower, a fluffy bath towel wrapped around her waist, Raleigh inventoried her closet with abject despair. Groaning, she sank her face into her palms. How had she let herself get roped into this? She'd meant to turn Dan down, but he'd looked so happy about the hunters, she hadn't had the heart to refuse him.

Now she was paying the price.

Her wardrobe consisted almost entirely of blue jeans and tank tops. She sighed heavily and slipped into her cotton bra and panties. Opening her closet, she realized that the few dresses she did own were hopelessly inappropriate. Raleigh tugged the despondent garments off the clothes rack and discarded one after the other onto her unmade bed.

The gauzy blue number she'd worn to the prom with Jack. No way. A red-and-green velvet Christmas creation Fay had given her five years ago. Wrong season. A rainbow-colored sundress. Too casual. And the black linen outfit she'd worn to Pa's funeral. Most definitely not.

She stared at the pathetic pile and threw her hands in the air. "That's it. I'm not going," she declared.

But despite her proclamation, she kept searching the confines of her closet until she located a gray circle skirt, and stepped into it. The delicate rayon garment flared softly around her legs. Rummaging further, she found the matching gray-and-white peasant blouse.

She'd purchased the ensemble last year to wear at Caleb's eighth-grade graduation. Frowning critically, she surveyed herself in the mirror, then added a wide black belt and knee-high black dress boots to the ensemble. Passable.

Perching on the edge of the bed, she peered into the mirror over her dressing table and applied a light streak of blusher to her cheeks. She dusted eye shadow across her lids, and dabbed on pearly pink lipstick. Usually, she never wore makeup, but as a concession to a trip into town, she even combed mascara through her lashes.

Removing the rubber band from the end of her braid, Raleigh brushed her hair until it tumbled down her shoulders in a cascade of crimped copper curls.

She stared at her reflection and sucked in a deep breath. No way. She looked far too eager. Raleigh started to braid her hair back up when a knock on the cabin door interrupted her.

Oh, dear. She wasn't ready for this. She didn't want to be alone with Daniel McClintock for even one minute, much less the whole evening.

He knocked again.

She abandoned the task of braiding her hair and went to answer the door.

Dan leaned casually against the doorjamb. He was hatless and had combed his thick black hair off his forehead. He wore sharply creased jeans and an azure blue silk shirt that complemented his dark coloring.

His mouth dropped open and his eyes grew wide as he stared at her with unabashed amazement. "Excuse me," he said. "Do I have the right cabin? I'm looking for Miss Raleigh Travers."

"Dan," she said in an exasperated tone. "Stop teasing." The telltale flush spreading up her neck made him grin. He'd embarrassed her. Good.

She looked like a glorious wildflower in full bloom with her unruly red hair corkscrewing down her back, the dove gray skirt swirling sexily around her slender but sturdy legs, her natural beauty defined and enhanced by the application of cosmetics. Absolutely breathtaking.

A woman to change your life for, Dan, he thought.

Nervously, Raleigh cleared her throat and brought a hand to her neck. "I've been thinking..." she began.

"You weren't planning on backing out on me, were you?" he asked. He clasped his hand to the left side of his chest. "It'll break my heart."

"We could have dinner at Fay's. We don't have to go to Abilene."

"No," he said. "We don't. But we're going to."

Not giving her time to protest further, he possessively took her hand, led her outside into the waning warmth of early evening and around to the passenger side of his pickup. He knew if he allowed her even one instant to ponder this date, she'd change her mind and retreat.

He enjoyed squiring her on his arm, knew it was a feeling he could get used to real quick. For weeks he'd tried his best to remain distant, detached, but now he could no longer deny the need she caused to flame inside him. To ignore that would be like ignoring the change of seasons. But how to reach her without scaring her off? Surely someone or something in her past had hurt her very badly, destroyed her ability to trust, and Dan was itching to know who or what.

Climbing into the front seat, Dan started the engine. Awkwardness stole over them. It was only the second time they'd been alone together since she'd moved into his cabin. Restlessly he drummed his fingers on the dashboard, then fiddled with the radio dials until he found a station to his liking. The country twang of Clint Black's guitar eased the uncomfortable silence in the cab.

Raleigh brushed a lock of hair from her eyes and sneaked a peek at him. His face claimed a stunning profile—long, angular jaw, regal nose, strong chin. The urge to run her hand over his chiseled features tempted her fingertips.

Wrenching her gaze away, she stared out over the hood, watching the yellow highway stripes disappear between the pickup's tires. Clint Black gave way to Garth Brooks. Dan rested his right hand on her knee.

"Relax," he said.

Sparks hot as a welder's torch zoomed up her thigh, igniting a flash fire of desire in her groin. Lord, what this man could do to her with a simple touch.

"Please remove your hand." Her voice came out in a timid squeak instead of the harsh command she'd intended.

He jerked back as if burned. "Sorry," he mumbled, keeping his eyes trained on the road. "But you had such a death grip on the door handle, I wanted to make you feel more comfortable. Look, your knuckles are blanched white."

"Oh." Feeling foolish, she released the door handle.

"I promise, I don't bite," he said.

"I'm not so sure about that," she replied tartly, struggling to tame her seething emotions.

"Do you want to talk about it?"

"Talk about what?"

"Your fear of being alone with me. Are you scared of losing control? Is that it?"

"I'm not afraid..." she started, then realized he was baiting her. "Can we change the subject."

"You see me as a threat, don't you?"

"Not at all," she lied.

"Then why are you so nervous about a simple dinner date?"

"It's not a date," she denied.

"Then what is it?"

He was right. It was a date. Oh, why had she agreed to come? Raleigh twisted a strand of hair around her index finger. A cross between elation and frustration welled up inside her. She truly liked Dan, but as she'd told herself over and over, she had to maintain a professional distance. First of all, her job depended on it. Second, she wasn't ready for a relationship with any man. Maybe she never would be. She heaved a heavy sigh.

"Are you okay?" Concern furrowed his brow.

"Fine."

"Raleigh, I'll never force you to do anything you're not comfortable with. Do you want me to turn this truck around and go back to the ranch?"

What to do? Since Jack's death she'd cocooned herself in anger and defensiveness, buffering her emotions by ignoring any and all sexual desires. Until Daniel McClintock, she'd had no trouble resisting temptation. In fact, he was the first man to ever renew her zest for the physical side of love. His power was terrifying, his very nearness inherently dangerous.

On the other hand, shouldn't she be able to have dinner with a handsome man without it turning into anything more complicated than a shared meal?

"Well?" he asked.

"I'm all right."

"You sure?"

"Uh-huh."

"So what would you like to eat? Chinese? Mexican? A steak?" he asked.

"Mexican food sounds good."

They entered the Abilene city limits and drove for a while. Dan stopped the pickup outside a quaint little restaurant. It was just before the dinner hour, but already the parking lot was crowded. The sun dipped low in the sky, heralding darkness.

The sounds of a mariachi band and the smell of corn tortillas filled the air. Neon lights blinked red, blue, green. Car doors slammed. Raleigh took a deep breath and, for one crazy moment, felt contented. It *had* been a long time since she'd been to the city or eaten in a restaurant. It felt good to get out.

Turning off the radio, Dan cut the engine and glanced over at her. "Now, you stay put until I get around to the other side."

She started to protest, but he'd already leapt out of the front seat and was running around to open the passenger-side door for her.

As she got out, the tip of her boot hung on the hem of her long skirt. Gasping, she found herself barreling forward right into his Dan's waiting arms.

"Whoa, there," he said, snagging her as she fell.

Her face flamed scarlet. "I—I'm sorry."

He held her aloft, inches from the ground. She could feel the power of the corded muscles in his forearm. His face hovered before hers, his dark eyes gleaming. She could smell his minty breath, the spicy scent of his cologne.

For one spontaneous second she thought he might kiss her, but the moment passed and he set her gently on the ground. Unexpectedly, disappointment nestled in her stomach.

"Let's go inside," he rasped, and that's when she realized what supreme effort of will it had taken for him not to claim her lips as his own.

Meekly, she followed him inside, feeling dazed by the vital undercurrent rippling between them. Blinking, she squinted against the cheerful brightness. A smiling hostess greeted them at the door, led them to their table and took their drink orders.

Dan held out a chair for her. Awkwardly, Raleigh sat down, and watched him settle in across from her.

"The Juarez Platter is excellent," he recommended, studying the menu.

"Fine," she said hoarsely. Food was the last thing on her mind.

Dan cracked his knuckles. He appeared as disconcerted as she felt.

The waitress returned with their drinks, setting a beer in front of Dan and a glass of ice tea before Raleigh.

"You're awfully quiet," he said.

"I don't know what to say." She watched him stroke a finger around the rim of his long-necked beer bottle. He had large, capable hands. The hands of a workman, tanned and callused. She wondered what it would feel like to have those hands caressing her naked flesh.

"Me, neither," he said. "You've got me quaking in my boots."

"I do?" His confession relaxed her a little. Big, strong Dan was nervous, too?

"Every time I look at you, I get a lump in my throat. You look so beautiful."

Raleigh struggled to control the heated rush seeping up her neck, and failed miserably. Blushing—the curse of the redhead.

"I want to propose a toast." He lifted his bottle.

"A toast?" She followed suit and raised her glass.

"To the best darn farrier in Texas."

"I guess I can drink to that." She grinned and clinked the lip of her glass against his beer bottle.

Their gazes met and held.

The steady, patient look in his eyes made her think of soft, sensual things—whispered moans, flower blossoms, delicate evening breezes, swaying bodies. In her mind she saw Dan's fingertips glide over her skin like wind rustling through mesquite branches.

She jerked her gaze away. The waitress arrived with their food. Relief swamped Raleigh. Keeping her head down, she concentrated on the meal of chicken enchiladas, soft cheese tacos, refried beans and Spanish rice.

"I like seeing you eat so heartily," Dan commented. "A woman with an appetite." He raised an eyebrow and she knew he referred to much more than food.

She didn't know what to say, but she knew she shouldn't encourage his behavior. They were only having dinner, period. She would do well to remain mindful of that fact.

"Dessert?" their waitress asked, gathering up their empty plates.

"What I want isn't on the menu," Dan said, looking squarely at Raleigh.

"Excuse me, sir?" asked the puzzled waitress.

"Never mind." He held up a palm. "Would you like some dessert, Raleigh?"

She placed a hand on her stomach and shook her head. "Too full." Truthfully, she wanted to get home so she could sort out her conflicting thoughts in private.

"No, thanks, miss." Dan smiled at the waitress. "We'll just take the check."

They left the restaurant and Raleigh glanced at her watch. Only seven-thirty? It seemed an eternity had passed instead of a few hours. Relieved to have the evening over with, Raleigh hurried to the truck without waiting for Dan to catch up.

Once they were inside the pickup, he keyed the ignition and headed out of town. Glancing over at him, Raleigh found herself wondering what thoughts crossed his mind.

"Where are we going?" Raleigh asked, noticing they hadn't taken the rode back to Clyde.

"I thought we might drive around the lake for a bit. It's a beautiful night."

"I don't think that's such a good idea. I'd really like to go home."

"Why? You chicken to be alone with me in the dark?"

Oh, yes. Yes.

"I'm not chicken," she denied. "I'm tired. I got up at the crack of dawn."

"It's not even eight o'clock yet," Dan said, slowing down at the cutoff. "I thought maybe we could talk awhile."

She didn't want to discuss feelings or share secrets or get to know Dan better, because she feared the results such intimacy would bring.

He parked by the shore. "Please," he said. "For me?"

"Dan..."

IT'S FUN! BIG BUCKS IT'S FREE!

HOW TO PLAY

It's so easy...grab a lucky coin, and go right to your BIG BUCKS game card. Scratch off silver squares in a STRAIGHT LINE (across, down, or diagonal) until 5 dollar signs are revealed. BINGO! Doing this makes you eligible for a chance to win $1,000,000.00 in lifetime income ($33,333.33 each year for 30 years). Also scratch all 4 corners to reveal the dollar signs. This entitles you to a chance to win the $50,000.00 Extra Bonus Prize! Void if more than 9 squares scratched off.

Your EXCLUSIVE PRIZE NUMBER is in the upper right corner of your game card. Return your game card and we'll activate your unique Sweepstakes Number, so it's important that your name and address section is completed correctly. This will permit us to identify you and match you with any cash prize rightfully yours! (SEE BACK OF BOOK FOR DETAILS.)

FREE BOOKS PLUS FREE GIFTS!

At the same time you play your BIG BUCKS game card for BIG CASH PRIZES...scratch the Lucky Charm to receive FOUR FREE

Silhouette Romance™ novels, and a FREE GIFT, TOO! They're totally free, absolutely free with no obligation to buy anything!

These books have a cover price of $2.99 each. But THEY ARE TOTALLY FREE; even the shipping will be at our expense! The Silhouette Reader Service™ is not like some book clubs. You don't have to make any minimum number of purchases–not even one!

The fact is, thousands of readers look forward to receiving six of the best new romance novels each month and they love our discount prices!

Of course you may play BIG BUCKS for cash prizes alone by not scratching off your Lucky Charm, but why not get everything that we are offering and that you are entitled to! You'll be glad you did.

Offer limited to one per household and not valid to current Silhouette Romance™ subscribers. All orders subject to approval.

▼ DETACH AND MAIL CARD TODAY! ▼

BIG BUCKS

EXCLUSIVE PRIZE # 3K 996960

	$			

HURRY!
This Jackpot must be claimed!
Scratch Here ↓

LUCKY CHARM GAME!

Claim 4 FREE books AND a FREE Mystery Gift!

YES! I have played my BIG BUCKS game card as instructed. Enter my Big Bucks Prize number in the MILLION DOLLAR Sweepstakes III and also enter me for the Extra Bonus Prize. When winners are selected, tell me if I've won. If the Lucky Charm is scratched off, I will also receive everything revealed, as explained on the back of this page.

215 CIS AS3L
(U-SIL-R-07/95)

NAME _____

ADDRESS _____ APT. ____

CITY _____ STATE _____ ZIP _____

NO PURCHASE OR OBLIGATION NECESSARY TO ENTER SWEEPSTAKES.

© 1993 HARLEQUIN ENTERPRISES LTD.   **PRINTED IN U.S.A.**

TWO WAYS TO WIN BIG BUCKS!

1. Uncover 5 $ signs in a row...BINGO! You're eligible for a chance to win the $1,000,000.00 SWEEPSTAKES!

2. Uncover 5 $ signs in a row AND uncover $ signs in all 4 corners...BINGO! You're also eligible for a chance to win the $50,000.00 EXTRA BONUS PRIZE!

He reached over and took her hand. "Let's go for a walk."

Raleigh gulped. Her emotions warred. Instinct cried for her to flee, and besides, she hated lakes. But good, old-fashioned lust tempted her to stay.

"Raleigh?"

She drew in a shaky breath. "Just for a minute."

They walked to the lake's edge, fingers interlaced. Her small hand felt protected by his large, capable one. And right now she craved security and safety because just looking at the murky water turned her stomach.

A crescent moon shone down on them, bathing Raleigh in a glow of shimmering white light. Her crimped red curls tumbled in sexy disarray down her slender shoulders. Dan swallowed, mesmerized by the sight.

She's so lovely, he thought, his gaze trailing down Raleigh's swanlike neck. He hadn't realized just how breathtaking she could be. A fairy-tale princess come to life for him. For once, she looked soft, tiny and vulnerable. He wanted to cradle her in his arms and promise to keep her safe for the rest of her life.

"Are you cold?" he asked, noticing her shivering.

She shook her head.

The plaintive sound of a whippoorwill echoed eerily, the water resonating the bird's tragic, lonely refrain. They stood together, watching the black waves lap against the shoreline. On the distant highway, cars whizzed by. Crickets chirped and bullfrogs croaked. The air smelled of earth and moistness, rich, fertile, life producing.

"I thought we might talk," Dan said. "Away from the ranch and our boss-employee relationship. I'd like to get to know you better."

"What's the point?" she asked, withdrawing her hand from his and wrapping her arms around herself.

"The point is, I'm interested, concerned. You've had a very hard life, haven't you?" he whispered.

"I don't want to discuss it."

Perhaps if he revealed things to her about his own childhood, she might reciprocate and open up to him. "Okay, then," he said. "If you won't talk to me, I'll tell you about my past.

"I'm the youngest of three sons. My father is the owner of McClintock Plastics. He manufactures the largest supply of PVC pipes in the state of Texas," Dan continued.

"Are you trying to tell me your father's loaded?"

"My family has money, yes."

"So why don't you just ask him for the money to renovate your ranch? And pay me a salary while you're at it?" Raleigh remarked.

Dan let out a harsh laugh. "And admit I'd failed already? He'd love that. No. I've finally managed to break free from his overpowering influence and I refuse to go back."

"I take it your father is the controlling type, huh?"

"Controlling is a gross understatement. He's the original control freak. He forced all his sons to go into the business. He even picked out and bought houses for my two brothers, Mike and Jamie, and their families. Whatever father wants, father gets, and nobody ever had the courage to stand against him. But I was suffocating living his life instead of my own."

"So you bought the ranch to escape?" Raleigh tilted her face upward.

"Running a ranch was the only thing I had ever wanted. He warned me I'd fail. He laughed and called me an idiotic dreamer. But I saved my money and got out. I had to prove myself, show him I could succeed on my own merits."

"You'll do it," she said.

"What makes you say so?"

"Because I'm here to help you."

"Is that really true, Raleigh? Will you stay on at the ranch and help me?" His voice caressed her. Raleigh raised her chin and looked into eyes the murky color of aged whiskey. Softly he rubbed her chin with a thumb and forefinger. "I care about you."

"Please, don't." She pressed her hands to her ears. "I don't want to hear this, Dan."

"Why not? Why do you insist on hiding from me?"

"It's nothing personal. I like you, but life's easier without complications."

"And I'm a complication, is that it?"

"Look, I'm trying my best to raise my teenage brother. It's all I have the time or energy for. Okay?"

"You're using Caleb as an excuse," he challenged.

"I'm not ready for a relationship at this point in my life. I might never be."

"You could try trusting me."

"Trust isn't my greatest strength."

"You're risking missing out on something special," he warned.

"Empty promises," she replied, her voice sounding cynical and bitter even to her own ears. "I've heard them before."

"From whom? I want to know. I want to share your pain. Let me be strong for you, Raleigh. Let me help shoulder your burdens the way you shoulder mine."

He moved closer, but she took a step backward, crushing a rotted log beneath her feet. Her breath came in short, rapid gasps.

"Oh, Dan," she said.

"May I kiss you, Raleigh Travers?"

She meant to say no, to turn and run back to the truck. Every nerve in her body shouted for her to go before she lost control. But it was too late. Her arms reached out for him, she stood on tiptoe, waiting.

He groaned and slipped an arm around her waist. He pressed his lips to her ear. "Say yes, Raleigh."

She whimpered. His masculine scent aroused her. His lips tempted. His daring gaze met hers, stark and knowing. She felt overwhelmed, as if he could read the secrets of her very soul.

"I won't kiss you without your permission. Say yes."

When he pulled her closer, she didn't resist. Instead she welcomed his embrace, enveloping herself in the intimate contact like a child sinking into a feather bed.

"Yes," she whispered, trembling.

Their lips joined, fused. She tasted his warm, moist mintiness. She inhaled the scent of autumn clinging to his skin.

"Oh, sweetheart." He sighed. Desire rampaged through him with the force of stampeding horses. Undiluted passion spilled from her lips. He felt the sizzling current, pure and electric, complete the circuit they'd created. Sharp, aching need rose in him and he realized no one but Raleigh could ever quench this particular thirst.

She lifted her hands and, for one instant, he feared she might push him away, but instead her arms encircled his neck, drawing him closer. At last, he'd broken through to her. At last, she surrendered to him.

As the kiss deepened, Dan felt his restraint slip. She moaned delicately into his mouth. He absorbed her noise, savored it. Cupping the back of her head in the palm of his hand, he held her close, exploring every nook and cranny of her exquisite haven.

Finally he tugged his lips from hers and mined a path of well-placed kisses down the length of her long neck. She wove her fingers through his dark hair and sighed her pleasure.

Dan experienced a desperate need to see her eyes, to read her emotions, to understand how she felt. Pulling back, he cupped her precious face in his hands.

The woman who stared back at him was no longer the stubborn, bristly female farrier he'd first hired. In her place stood a softhearted, vulnerable young woman who badly needed his love.

"Raleigh," he said, "I could hold you forever."

In an instant the old Raleigh returned, a veiled, hunted look clouding her eyes. Her hands trembled. She pushed hard against his chest.

"Stop," she cried.

"What's wrong? What did I say?"

Twisting from his grasp, she leapt away. What on earth had she been thinking? She staggered back to the truck, anxious to distance herself from Daniel McClintock and his bewitching kisses. Had she lost her ever-loving mind? She must be crazy—mad! What had come over her? She'd never behaved so irrationally in her entire life.

Raleigh shrank back against the pickup as Dan approached her. The chilled metal beneath her thin cotton blouse sent goose bumps racing up her spine. Dan appeared confused—and small wonder. One minute she ran hot as the town floozy. The next minute, colder than a blue norther. Her heart fluttered; she puffed like a marathoner running that last mile.

"Raleigh? What's wrong? What did I do to frighten you?"

"This is insane."

"Sweetheart, if what I'm feeling for you is insanity, then I want to be crazy forever."

"Don't call me sweetheart."

"I'm sorry."

"Take me home," she said.

Fumbling open the door, she hopped inside and buried her face in her hands. She forced herself to take slow, deep breaths. Just when things were going smoothly, Dan had spoiled everything by kissing her. No, she thought miserably. That wasn't true. She was as much to blame. More so. She'd allowed it, encouraged him.

Need burned in her, ripe and raw, provoking feelings she'd thought lost for good. Feelings of gentleness, hope and longing. Serious feelings that scared her.

Her bottom lip trembled. Raleigh lifted a hand to her mouth, softly fingering the tender flesh so recently branded by Dan's fiery signature.

She registered Dan slipping behind the wheel and starting the truck. He cleared his throat but said nothing.

Turbulent inner emotions disturbed her so deeply, Raleigh couldn't bear to look at him for fear she might do or say something she would regret.

What to do? She couldn't escape the inevitable consequences of their kiss. She wanted him physically. Period. It was that simple and that complicated.

If she stayed at the ranch, sooner or later she would succumb to these feelings and submit her body to him. She knew it as surely as birds migrate south for the winter.

Distracted, she closed her eyes and willed her mind to think clearly. Silence engulfed them. Acutely conscious of Dan's raspy breathing, Raleigh found her own chest rising and falling in perfect accompaniment to his labored rhythm.

Oh, this was too awful. How could she continue to live at the ranch after this? She'd made a tragic error in agreeing to come on this ill-fated date.

On the other hand, how could she afford to leave? Especially now. She had nowhere else to turn, no place to live, no other job. Besides, Dan needed her. That much was obvious.

But if she stayed, she'd be opening herself up to the very real possibility of greater pain and suffering. She couldn't survive another lost love. Not again. She absolutely refused to fall in love with Daniel McClintock.

Raleigh stared unseeingly out the window, her mind locked in a morass of quandary and indecision. Was it possible to give her body to him without involving her heart? Could she surrender physically while remaining emotionally detached?

The idea both excited and disgusted her, to think she was capable of using him like that. But then, she'd never before experienced such strong sensual yearnings, hadn't realized such passion existed. Even Jack hadn't been able to arouse her the way Daniel McClintock could.

"Raleigh?" Dan asked, his voice tight with cracking tension.

"Yes?"

"You're not thinking about leaving the ranch over this, are you?"

"I don't know," she answered honestly.

"Please," he said. "Look at me."

Raleigh turned her head, found herself looking up into his dark, shining eyes, and then she knew. The sexual force brewing between them was as destructive and inescapable as a relentless tidal wave.

"I need you. I don't know if I can make a go of the ranch without you," he whispered.

In that long, suspense-filled moment, Raleigh made her decision. She would stay at the ranch and let the horseshoes fall where they may.

Chapter Seven

They decided to have an autumn fling. It would be a combination barbecue, barn dance and hayride designed to welcome in the fall season and promote the ranch in the community.

They printed up flyers and took out advertising. Raleigh contacted churches, schools and civic groups, while Dan hired a well-known local country-and-western band, as well as a caterer from Abilene. The plan was to charge ten dollars a person and offer the biggest, blowout harvest party ever to hit Callaghan County.

After that memorable kiss on the night she and Dan went to Abilene, Raleigh had once again put their relationship on a purely professional footing. She became totally absorbed in preparations for the party, giving Dan little opportunity to corner her.

Confused by the powerful emotions struggling within her, she threw herself into her work, starting her busy day at 5:00 a.m. and collapsing into bed after 10:00 p.m. But despite her exhausting schedule, she couldn't stop herself from thinking about Dan and the seductive way he cocked his cowboy hat back on his head, or his self-confident swagger, or his rich masculine scent of leather and woodsmoke.

He even visited her dreams, haunting her, teasing her, causing her to wake in the middle of the night lonely and aching for the comfort of his arms.

There was no escaping the man now. She'd promised to help him raise money for the ranch and Raleigh Travers was a woman of her word. Her safest bet lay in making the best of the situation and keeping her erotic fantasies on a very tight leash. With any luck, she could get through this uncertain period in her life with her heart unscathed.

The Saturday of the party dawned crisp and clear. Delighted with the good weather, Raleigh hopped out of bed nervous and excited. Dressing quickly, she hurried to move the horses to the back pasture so she, Pete and Caleb could scrub down the barn before the band and caterers arrived that afternoon.

They'd readied the tractor-trailer rig for the hayride yesterday, and scattered the ranch with pumpkins, hay bales, lanterns and brightly colored streamers.

Dan had cordoned off an area for parking, and constructed a ticket booth for the cakewalk and bingo games they planned. Pete and Caleb erected dozens of picnic tables on the tennis court slab and installed Porta Potties to meet their guests' requirements.

Fay Walton had also volunteered to help with the festivities, even closing the diner for the day so she could participate. She arrived just after dawn, wearing a smile and carrying a box of doughnuts.

"You look fantastic," Fay told Raleigh, handing her a strawberry Danish. "Working out here suits you much better than slinging hash."

"Thanks," Raleigh replied, taking a bite of the sweet pastry. If only Fay knew the truth.

"She does look great, doesn't she?" Dan said, grinning. He joined them beside the barn, toting a broom and shovel in his hands.

Raleigh blushed. Looking away, she avoided Fay's inquisitive stare. She knew all of Clyde was speculating about her relationship with Daniel McClintock, but she refused to satisfy their curiosity. They wouldn't believe her, anyway.

"Fay," Dan said, "I'm putting you in charge of the caterers. If you'll follow me, I'll show you around."

Breathing a sigh of relief at their departure, Raleigh finished her pastry, dusted her fingers on the seat of her pants, and pulled on a pair of work gloves. She retrieved the shovel Dan had discarded and busied herself scooping horse droppings from the barn floor.

Hard work never bothered her, nor the pungent aroma of horses. Chester stayed at her side and several times she had to shoo the bothersome dog out the door. By the time Dan returned with Pete and Caleb, she'd halfway completed the task.

"Hold on," Dan said, resting a hand on her shoulder. "You don't have to tackle this alone."

His touch caused her heart to roller coaster in her chest. Forcefully, she struggled to keep her expression impassive.

"Take a break." His gloved hand closed over hers and he pried the shovel from her grasp.

Her mouth went dry; her stomach tingled. She shouldn't have eaten that Danish, she thought, trying lamely to ex-

plain her body's reaction to the intensity of Dan's steady
gaze. No matter how much she might prefer to deny it,
even being near the man made her weak-kneed and addle
brained.

Blindly she grabbed for the push broom leaning against
the wall, and shoved it across the barn floor toward the
open door.

Dan bent over to pick up some collected debris and to
her abject horror, Raleigh found herself eyeing his firm
backside. Everything he did, every move he made, created
electric friction inside her.

The ensuing hours were pure torture as they worked side
by side. She'd glance over and see his sinewy muscles rippling beneath his shirt or his tanned forearms bunching
like coiled wire. His manly vigor entranced her, in spite of
her vow to remain cool and detached.

They finished cleaning the barn at noon. Fay carried a
platter full of sandwiches to the patio and called to them
that lunch was ready.

Turning to wash up at the outdoor sink, Raleigh crashed
full-on into Dan's chest. Flustered, she jumped back,
stumbling over a feed bucket.

"Whoa, there," Dan said, putting out an arm to steady
her. His deep voice echoed in the confines of the empty
barn. Raleigh felt dizzy, disoriented. Closing her eyes
briefly, she swallowed hard.

"You okay?" he asked.

"Fine. Fine," she mumbled, stepping up to the sink,
shedding her work gloves and vigorously soaping her
hands.

Dan stood next to her, unmoving. Why wouldn't he go
away? She could feel the warmth of his breath on the top
of her head. Shivering, she shifted to one side. His close-
ness affected her irrationally.

"Place looks real nice," he observed, surveying the barn over his shoulder. "And you deserve most of the credit."

Dan noticed she held her shoulders stiff and her head high in that proud, defensive manner of hers. What would it take to break down her barriers? That night by the lake he thought his kisses had chiseled a tiny chink in her protective armor. Had he been wrong?

What would it take to get through to her? Would she ever learn to trust? For the millionth time he wondered what had happened to her in the past to make her rebuff him at every opportunity.

After their magical, spellbinding date, Dan had believed things would be different between them, but he'd been wrong. If anything, Raleigh seemed more unapproachable than ever, withdrawing into her work, keeping him at bay, avoiding interaction with him as much as possible. Her response saddened and perplexed him.

She stalked across the yard to the house, and Dan followed her with his eyes, admiring her springy purposeful step, appreciating her trademark braid, approving of her tight, compact caboose. Sexual hunger chewed at him, instant and intense.

Damn, but the woman did dangerous things to him. Well, Miss Raleigh Travers had been denying her needs too long. Tonight, at the party, Dan was determined to dance with her and snuggle against her on the hayride whether she wanted him to or not. He'd kept his distance before, but now it was time he took charge and made her face her feelings and the troublesome past that prevented her from enjoying the present.

Sighing, Dan joined the others on the patio. They ate ham sandwiches and drank lemonade. He'd hoped to sit next to Raleigh, but somehow she'd managed to maneuver Caleb between them.

"All the kids at school are talking about the party," Caleb said. "I think it's going to be a big success."

"I hope so," Dan responded.

"Maybe we could turn the barn into a haunted house for Halloween and charge admission. What do you think, Dan?" The boy grinned, obviously eager for male approval.

"Why, I think that's an excellent idea, don't you, Raleigh?" Dan asked.

"Huh?" Raleigh replied, distracted from her reverie. Looking up from her plate, she found Caleb, Dan, Pete and Fay all staring at her.

"Caleb thought we could turn the barn into a haunted house for Halloween. I think it's a great idea," Dan repeated, raising an eyebrow in her direction.

"It would take a lot of work," Raleigh mused. "And money."

Dan draped his arm across Caleb's shoulders, and Raleigh experienced a jealous twinge at their obvious friendship.

Since she and her brother had moved into the log cabin, Caleb and Dan had formed a great camaraderie. Often, in the evenings, Caleb would slip off to the big house and play video games or watch action-adventure movies on Dan's VCR.

And she had to admit, Dan was good for the boy. He took Caleb horseback riding and talked to him man-to-man. Her brother confided in Dan, admitting hopes and fears he would never have verbalized to her. Dan had even taught Caleb how to drive Pete's old work truck around the ranch perimeters. Their budding relationship had deepened to the point where Raleigh felt a little shut out.

"Trust sis to be practical," Raleigh heard Caleb whisper to Dan. "She never has any fun."

His words hit her with the cold slap of truth. Her stomach knotted. She *didn't* have fun. Hadn't in a long time. Hard work and responsibility at a young age prevented it. She was boring and practical and staid.

Raleigh got up from the picnic table, wadding her empty paper plate in her hand. She tossed it in a nearby trash can, and tried hard to breathe past the lump in her throat. Aware of everyone's gaze upon her, she faked nonchalance. Taking her sunglasses from her front shirt pocket, she slipped them on to disguise the hurt in her eyes.

"Looks like the caterers are here," she said coolly, pointing at the driveway.

The group broke up. Fay and Dan went to deal with the caterers, while Pete, Raleigh and Caleb started decorating the barn.

They filled brightly colored balloons with helium and watched them bob gracefully to the ceiling. They hung orange and brown crepe-paper streamers and tacked a large Welcome banner across the front of the barn. They placed yellow tablecloths on the picnic tables and added bouquets of fall flowers.

Two hours later the band arrived, along with some high school students Dan had hired to take tickets and direct traffic. It was after five o'clock by the time Raleigh trudged to the log cabin to clean up and change for the party.

Indulging herself, she took a leisurely bath instead of her usual shower. It helped her to relax, and if she was going to survive this night, she needed to be as peaceful as possible. She twisted her hair into an elegant French knot, and dressed in a blue gingham dress she'd bought the day before. Dabbing on a light dusting of makeup, she added a squirt of lilac cologne before stepping outside into the noisy hubbub.

The McKary Brothers band tuned up, vibrating the air with melodious chords. Chester streaked through the exercise yard, tongue hanging out, while Caleb unfolded lawn chairs around the patio.

Near the tennis courts, the caterers had started grilling; a bossy chef carefully orchestrated the project. Delicious smells greeted her nose. Hot dogs and sausages lined one grill, ribs and brisket roasted on another, while a third held sizzling hamburgers.

Card tables sagged beneath the weight of potato salad, coleslaw, fruit compotes, relish trays and vats of baked beans. To one side, six ice-cream makers toiled diligently, grinding salty ice into delectable frozen treats.

Raleigh scanned the gathering crowd, searching for Dan's tall figure. Where was he? she wondered, feeling lost without his steady support.

Dodging extension cords and other equipment, Raleigh picked her way across the yard to the barn. Nervousness tightened her gut. She hated crowds, rarely socialized, and always felt inept at parties. She turned to flee back to the safety of her cabin but found Dan blocking her way.

Her heart jumped.

"You look good enough to eat." His voice spilled over her like a creamy chocolate confection—dark, rich, and sinfully delicious.

She liked the way his eyes crinkled at the corners; it made him appear friendly, approachable, like someone she could tell all her secrets to.

Where did that last thought come from? Raleigh shook her head. She didn't want to discuss her past with anyone, much less Daniel McClintock.

"Hello," she said primly, casting her gaze around the milling crowd. "Is there anything I can help with?"

"Stay next to me." He took her hand and squeezed. "Remember, this is our project and I need you."

"I'm not much of a party girl, I'm afraid. If that's what you're used to."

Dan stroked her cheek with the back of his index finger. The sensation sent tingling messages flooding through her neurons.

"I don't want a party girl," he whispered low and husky. "I want you."

"Why would you want me? I'm boring," she said. "Haven't you heard? Even my kid brother thinks so."

"Caleb didn't mean anything by that remark. He just wants to see you happy. And *I* happen to think you're the most intricate, fascinating woman I've ever known. You elude me, Raleigh. I only want to understand."

"Shouldn't we mingle with the guests?" she interrupted, anxious to change the subject. She did not want to hear his words, realizing how close she was to weakening, to giving up and accepting the inevitable.

"Dan! How you doin'?" Jerry Hanks from the feed store called out. "Where you hidin' the suds, old buddy?"

"Got a designated driver tonight, Jer?"

"Sure do, brought my missus, Arlene. She's 'round here somewhere, gabbing it up."

"In that case, follow me," Dan said, escorting Jerry over to the iced keg.

The next few hours passed in a blur of activity. Buzzing voices mixed with the scent of grilling meat, infusing the growing twilight with a down-home quality. Folks laughed, joked, talked. The sound of slamming car doors heralded more visitors.

Dan greeted the guests with hearty handshakes and enthusiastic words of welcome, but all the while he kept one arm securely draped across Raleigh's shoulders. It felt good resting there, she grudgingly admitted to herself, and for the first time in many weeks, she started to relax.

Pete lit the lanterns, bathing the old ranch in a soft, romantic glow. The band broke into a slow, tear-jerking ballad about lost love.

"Have you had a chance to eat yet?" Dan whispered to her.

"No."

"Me, either. The line's thinned out, want to go grab a bite?"

"Sure."

They walked over to the grill and helped themselves to the buffet. Carrying plates loaded with food, they sat side by side at a vacated picnic table. Most of the livelier guests packed into the barn to dance, while the more sedate bunch sat in lawn chairs around the periphery.

"The party's going well," Dan observed. Light as a feather, his bare arm brushed her shoulder and his hard thigh pressed against her soft one.

Denim strumming cotton. Friction. The sensation evoked in Raleigh a sincere desire to sin.

Dan's teeth flashed white in the darkness.

A half-moon smiled wide across the velvet sky. Spicy barbecue lingered sweet yet tart on her tongue. Woodsmoke hung acrid in the air, and the ground beneath their feet vibrated with the power of a throbbing base. Raleigh tapped her toes in time to the music.

"Would you like a dish of homemade ice cream?" Dan asked after they'd finished their meal.

"Okay."

He stood and extended his hand. Letting her tranquil mood carry her along, Raleigh slipped her palm into his. Together they ambled over to the now-silent ice-cream makers.

Picking up plastic bowls from a nearby table, Dan opened the lid and dipped out homemade peach ice cream. Then they strolled over to the barn, helping themselves to spoonfuls of the creamy concoction.

Inside the barn, dancers promenaded to the "Cotton-Eyed Joe."

"You seem to be having a good time," Dan said. "I've never seen you look so serene."

"This *is* nice," she confessed.

"And it's only a start. Tonight has stoked my enthusiasm. I can't wait until the dude ranch is in full swing." His face brightened as he talked about his dream. Raleigh stared at him, mesmerized.

"It'll be wonderful," she said.

"Would you like to dance?" he asked.

No, her mind warned. *Not now.* She felt too vulnerable, too ripe for suggestion.

"I enjoy watching just fine, thanks."

"Come on. One dance won't kill you."

"I don't know about that," she replied, cautiously eyeing the boisterous dancers two-stepping across the hay-strewn floor.

"Yeah," Dan said. "You're right. Better not risk it, you might actually have some fun."

She swallowed the lump in her throat. He was right. She did shy away from a good time. As a young girl she'd been too busy accepting responsibilities to worry about having fun. The loss of her mother had robbed her of her childhood innocence, then Jack's death had brought her up short, stealing any of the carefree impulses she might once have possessed. And Pa's demise had only compounded her serious, practical nature.

Dan smiled. "Please, Raleigh, dance with me. For one night, let yourself go free."

"I can't. I don't know how to dance," she confessed.

"Well, darlin'," he drawled, thick and sexy. "You let me take care of everything."

Before she could protest further, Dan eased her through the crowd and onto the dance floor. Clutching her tightly, he angled his head down and whispered, "Follow my lead."

She clung to him, feeling nervous and out of her element. The disparity in their heights made dancing together almost comical. The top of her head grazed his shoulder.

"Regular Mutt and Jeff, aren't we?" Dan commented as if reading her thoughts.

"Yes. A bad match, indeed."

"When you're prone, darlin', height don't mean a thing." He chuckled.

With her ear pressed so close to his chest, she heard the distant rumble of his hearty laughter. Cursing the hot flush running up her neck, Raleigh moved her head. He certainly had a way of burrowing under her skin. And what was this "darlin'" stuff, anyway?

Gracefully, he guided her around the other dancers. She spied Fay and Pete dancing together. Fay caught her eye and winked. The crowd thickened, making it impossible to keep any distance between herself and Dan.

He held her close yet cautiously, as if she were rare porcelain. Raleigh wondered how many other women he'd held like this on a dance floor. Probably hundreds.

They swayed in time with the music and she felt the hard outline of his thigh bumping against her hip. He rested his cheek against her hair and sighed.

"Raleigh."

She raised her head and looked into his face. A sheen of perspiration dotted his upper lip. "Yes, Dan?"

"We've got to talk. In private."

"Not tonight."

"No," he agreed. "But soon."

He was right. They did need to talk. Things couldn't continue as they were. Something had to give between them and Raleigh would be damned if it was her heart.

The band burst into a fast-paced song.

"Ready to boogie?" Dan asked, spinning her breathlessly around the floor.

How could she hope to combat his relentless optimism? Raleigh wondered, knowing Dan possessed the ability to talk her into things she knew weren't prudent. Nothing daunted this man for long.

They shimmied and shook to the upbeat tune. Her head swam and she hung on to Dan, helpless as a rubber raft tossed adrift on wild ocean currents.

Raleigh practically floated in his arms. She was petite, dainty, and he wondered, not for the first time, how she managed to wrangle horses so well.

He knew he was walking on eggshells where their relationship was concerned. One false move and she'd disappear from his life like a plume of ephemeral smoke. Although she'd begun to change in the weeks she'd worked at the ranch, she still remained guarded, distant, veiling her true feelings with stubbornness and anger.

But tonight he sensed her staunch resolve weakening. Tonight could be the night he finally crashed through her defenses.

The crowd jostled them. He clung tighter to her hand, pulling her along with him. The soft rhythm of her breasts sliding across his torso drove him crazy with lust. He meshed his hips into hers, letting her know exactly how much she affected him.

"Will you go on the hayride with me?" he murmured into her perfectly shaped ear, his heart chugging at the thought of her refusal.

She looked up. Pain lodged in his midsection. Would she reject him?

"Please?"

Her full lips parted, he smelled the fruity scent of peaches on her breath. Tendrils of copper-colored hair drifted around her pixie face. When she lowered her gaze, long lashes brushed against her cheeks.

Anticipation gripped his chest, suspense stretched endlessly as he waited for her reply. Please let her say yes, he prayed.

"Ride with me tonight," he whispered. "Will you?"

Though a worried frown creased her brow, she nodded, ever so slightly.

"You will?" His eyes widened in surprise. He hadn't expected a positive response.

"Yes, Dan, I'll sit with you on the hayride. And stop looking so shocked."

"I...but...oh...never mind." He shut his mouth and grinned, feeling fifty pounds lighter. Did this mean what he hoped it meant? Had she just agreed to take their relationship one step farther?

She tossed her head back and laughed, a tinkling melodious sound that drove a spike of desire straight through to his groin. What a beautiful noise it was! A sound to be courted. A sound to be worshiped.

"What's so funny?" he asked.

"The look on your face is priceless." Mirth crinkled the corners of her lips. If only there was some way to cajole her into laughing more often.

"I'm glad I make you happy, sweetheart."

Her laughter died instantly, her sober, serious look returned. What had he said wrong?

The song ended and Raleigh sprang away from him. "It's time for the hayride," she said. "You should make an announcement."

Dan walked to the stage and moved to take the microphone. But his eyes never left Raleigh.

He cleared his throat and announced the end of the musical entertainment and the start of the hayride.

Stepping off the stage, he captured her gaze. He extended his hand to her and held his breath. When at last she settled her palm into his, Dan knew with absolute assurance that after tonight there could be no turning back for either of them.

The band disassembled while the crowd filtered outside. Some guests headed for their cars, others climbed into the back of the tractor-trailer rig piled high with musty hay. Pete fired up the tractor engine and honked the horn.

"Where's Caleb?" Raleigh asked.

"He's around here somewhere," Dan assured her.

"Maybe he'd like to go with us, too. He's worked so hard, I don't want to run off and leave him."

"There he is." Dan pointed.

She caught a glimpse of her brother sitting alone at an abandoned picnic table. Without waiting for Dan to follow, she scurried over to her brother. "Hey, you going on the hayride with us?"

Caleb grimaced. "Nah, my stomach hurts."

"Too much rich food," Dan diagnosed.

"Listen, Dan. I can't possibly go now," she said, feeling both relieved and disappointed.

"Oh, please, sis. Go on. I'll be fine. Fay's staying behind to help clean up. She can look after me."

Dan touched Raleigh's elbow. "He's a big boy, Raleigh. You've got to untie the apron strings sometime."

"You sure it's okay?" Torn between duty and a desire to snuggle with Dan on the hayride, she looked from Caleb to Dan and back again.

"Go. Have fun." Caleb shooed them with a wave of his hand. "Have you guys ever considered I might want you out of my hair?"

Pete honked again. "All aboard that's going aboard," he sang out.

"That's our ride," Dan cued.

Raleigh cast a worried glance over her shoulder at Caleb as Dan hauled her to the overcrowded trailer. Everyone shifted closer to make room, but it was a tight squeeze. Raleigh found herself sitting on Dan's lap, encircled by his muscular legs and pressed firmly against his lower anatomy. They fit together perfectly, like interconnecting cogs.

Someone pulled out a harmonica and began to play "Down in the Valley." The festive mood continued as everyone sang along. Dan's rich baritone blended with the other voices, yet stood alone, strong and distinct.

"'Angels in heaven know I love you,'" he sang, wrapping his arms around her waist. Raleigh leaned into him, savoring the happy moment she knew would never last.

Pete drove the rig across the pasture and soon they lost sight of the house. They lumbered over bumpy hills and several times she lurched into Dan's chest.

One song flowed into another. She tilted her head back and eyed the wide expanse of sky and stars.

"We created this," Dan whispered. "You and me and Pete and Caleb."

"Yes," she said. At this moment the world seemed made for them, but Raleigh knew just how short-lived joy could be. The minute she dropped her guard, took happiness for granted, trusted in the status quo, life dissolved into heart-wrenching tragedy. It had occurred again and again, teaching her severe lessons at an early age.

Pete reached the end of Dan's property and turned the trailer around. Couples cuddled. Mesquite loomed in the dark. An owl hooted. Hay and peanuts scented the breeze. Dan's wristwatch glowed green and she could hear the steady, reliable ticking.

The tractor labored, sending vibrations seeping through the bed of the trailer, flowing energy upward to invade her bottom with spirals of sensation. She shifted and wondered if Dan felt it, too. His grip on her waist tightened as they traveled to the house. Several guests yawned. The singing stopped and conversation lagged.

The rig ground to a halt in front of the barn. Guests hopped down, voicing their appreciation for the party and drifting in the direction of their vehicles. Raleigh started to get up, but Dan kept her restrained in his arms.

"Wait," he said. "Let them all leave."

Bidding their visitors good night, they sat planted in the comfortable hay, watching a succession of departing headlights sweep over the driveway. Dan plucked loose straw from her hair, feathering it gently across her cheek.

"That tickles." She giggled.

"I'd like to trail it over your whole body," he said.

Oh, heavens, she would like that, too!

"Well," Pete announced, climbing down from the tractor. "I'm turning in for the night." He grinned slyly.

"Good night, Pete," they chorused.

Chuckling, Pete shook his head and disappeared into the night.

Dan lay back in the hay and pulled Raleigh down beside him. His outstretched arm rested under her head. "Alone at last," he whispered.

"We're going to have one heck of a mess to clean up in the morning," Raleigh said.

"There you go again, obsessing about work. Relax. Clear your mind."

"Easier said than done."

"Skeptic," Dan replied, propping himself on one elbow and peering down at her. She knew he was going to kiss her, but she possessed no will to resist.

His lips sought hers, hungry, searching, demanding. His kiss escalated her passion, left her gasping for more.

Threading both hands through her hair, he held her face to his and delved deeper with his tongue, stoking the torch flaming inside her.

With the agility of a champion Thoroughbred, he rolled them over until his body covered hers like a saddle blanket. He kissed her again and again, expertly, intently, his lips promising so much more to come.

While his mouth occupied hers, his fingers smoothly undid the buttons on her dress, exposing the flesh beneath. The night breeze cooled her sizzling skin like a soothing balm. But then his large hands skimmed her rib cage, provoking a fresh cascade of heated longing.

"Raleigh, Raleigh, Raleigh," he crooned. His fingers released the catch on her bra and pushed the restraining material out of his way. Moaning deep in his throat, he cupped her breasts in his palms.

His deep, guttural sounds ignited her. Writhing under his touch, she cried his name, no longer aware of her surroundings, no longer caring. All that mattered was Dan and her body's starving response. She wanted him, needed him, but she was so afraid to surrender everything to him.

Wrenching his mouth from her lips, he trailed fire red kisses down her neck, teasing her with his tongue. Intense shivers rippled through her body as she arched her back and begged for more.

"You're so sweet." He sighed. Feverishly, he tore his shirt open, buttons popping into the hay with soft plopping sounds. He guided her hands to his bare chest. Her fingers splayed outward, massaging him, kneading him, arousing him to unbelievable heights.

She tugged gently at his chest hairs and he growled in answer. Angling her hips upward, she moved against him, felt his obvious arousal straining at his restrictive blue jeans. She whimpered, acutely aware of his masculine hardness.

Her hands clutched his shoulders and she savored the tactile experience of caressing his warm skin. What strange, mystical powers did Daniel McClintock possess that he could reduce her to a quivering mass of pure desire?

The pressure between them increased to a fever pitch. Jack's tender lovemaking had never aroused her to this level of wondrous ecstasy.

Jack. Thoughts of her ex-fiancé zapped through Raleigh's mind like a charged cattle prod.

Dear God, hadn't she learned her lesson? What was she thinking, succumbing to Dan in such a wanton way? Physical intimacy with this man made it so much harder to keep a rein on her emotions. And control her feelings she must, if she ever hoped to keep from destroying him and herself in the process.

She had to shut down her feelings and do it now while she still possessed enough strength to resist his overwhelming temptation. She simply could not afford to put Dan's life in jeopardy by loving him.

"Raleigh?" His fingers slowed, but continued to caress her bare skin.

She squirmed from his touch, agony ripping through her.

"Stop!" she cried, pushing against Dan's chest and heaving with all her might. He tumbled to one side. Sitting upright, she fumbled to fix her bra and close the buttons on her dress.

Dan sucked in ragged gasps of air. "What's wrong?" he asked, instantly attuned to her acute distress.

What had she done? She'd been such a fool to let things go this far!

At that very moment the porch light at the big house flashed on. Raleigh frowned. Pete should have been asleep by now. When the front door slammed, instant fear shot through her.

Pete came running down the steps, stumbling in his haste.

Suspecting the worst, she leapt from the back of the trailer. She knew a crisis when she saw it.

"Raleigh?" Dan rolled out behind her.

Flying at a dead run, she met Pete in the middle of the exercise yard. The older man's hands trembled violently, his weathered face blanched deathly pale.

"What is it Pete? What's wrong?" She grabbed his shoulders, shook him.

"Come quick," he finally managed.

"What's wrong!" she shouted.

"It's Caleb. He's real sick. Oh, Raleigh, I think he might be dying!"

Chapter Eight

Raleigh clutched a hand to her heart. She tore across the yard, heading for the house, Pete and Dan at her heels.

"Caleb!" she cried, pushing through the front door and spying her little brother doubled over on Dan's sofa.

Kneeling beside him, she gathered him into her arms and rested his head on her shoulders. She brushed a copper-colored strand of hair from his eyes.

"What's wrong, honey?"

"Sis," he whispered. "I hurt so bad." Trying to be brave, he blinked back a tear, his bottom lip quivering.

"Where does it hurt?" She felt blood rush to her head, her temples pounded. Dizziness assailed her. She swayed beneath his weight, struggled to remain calm.

"Here." Caleb clutched the right side of his lower abdomen.

"He's got to be taken to the hospital," Dan broke in, grabbing his hat off the peg by the door and slamming it onto his head. "Immediately."

Dazed, her mind numb with terror, she nodded.

Bending over, Dan scooped Caleb from Raleigh's arms and started out the front door. Temporary paralysis rendered her actionless. Like a helpless bystander, she watched Dan take her only surviving family member away from her. Oh, dear God, she couldn't lose Caleb. Not him, too.

"Raleigh." Dan called to her from the open door. "Come on." Jumping to her feet, she grabbed an afghan from the back of the sofa and ran after them.

"Should I come?" Pete asked, his face twisted with worry.

"Stay here and look after the place," Dan commanded, stalking purposefully toward his truck.

Why, oh, why, had she gone on that damnable hayride? Raleigh thought. If she'd stayed home with her brother where she'd belonged, she would have been there for him when he'd needed her most. But she'd been in the back of the tractor-trailer rig making love to Daniel McClintock.

Self-loathing swelled inside her. She blamed herself for everything. Had she been insane? She'd known better than to let Dan get close to her. Look what had happened the minute she'd started to care for him!

"Raleigh, open the door," Dan said patiently. His arm muscles bulged from the effort of holding her husky, fourteen-year-old brother aloft.

Caleb moaned. Raleigh wrenched open the door and stood back while Dan rested Caleb inside. She scooted in beside her brother and Dan took the wheel.

"What were you doing at Dan's house?" Raleigh asked Caleb. Looking down, she was appalled to find she'd buttoned her dress incorrectly. She quickly redid the buttons, hoping Caleb hadn't noticed.

"I wanted to play video games," he whispered, pressing a hand to his abdomen. "But I felt too bad."

"Why didn't you tell Fay?"

"I didn't want to bother her. I thought it would go away. So I waited for you to come back from the hayride."

Guilt's vicious claws tore into her. She looked over at Dan, and saw that his lips were flattened into a grim line. If only she hadn't succumbed to his charms and had stayed behind in the house with Caleb. He shifted the pickup into reverse and rocketed out of the driveway, spewing gravel.

"It hurts," Caleb whimpered, and drew a sharp breath.

"Shh ... don't talk."

What would she do if something happened to Caleb? Panic dashed through her at the awful thought. Her mouth went dry. No. She refused to consider that possibility. Nothing was going to happen to him. He would be fine. She had to believe that.

"You hanging in there?" Dan glanced over at her. Although she laid part of the blame at his feet, she was glad to have him here, on her side.

She nodded. Caleb's head flopped back and she braced him against her shoulder. He felt so hot.

"I'm tired," her brother mumbled, and put out his tongue to moisten his lips.

Dan trod on the accelerator and belatedly turned on the headlights. "Hang in there, kid," he soothed.

"I can't seem to get enough air." Caleb sighed.

Raleigh rolled down the window. "Lean your head over this way and take some deep breaths."

"You always know what to do, sis."

No, not always, she thought, shooting another look in Dan's direction. If she'd known what she was doing, she would have left the ranch the very first time Daniel McClintock had kissed her.

Dan turned off the graveled road, guided the truck onto the entrance ramp and hit the highway. The nearest hospital was in Abilene, twenty miles away. It might as well be two hundred, Raleigh thought dismally.

Perspiration lay thick on her brother's upper lip. Raleigh smoothed the moisture away with her sleeve. Dan drove faster. The pickup shimmied in response. Raleigh hoped they'd meet a police cruiser, but no such luck.

The lights of Abilene sparkled in the distance, a welcoming beacon. So close and yet so far. What would happen if Caleb didn't make it in time? Raleigh shook her head. She couldn't afford the luxury of negative thoughts. If she gave in to that horrible conclusion, she would break down completely and Caleb was depending on her.

"Everything is going to be all right," Dan told her, as if reading her thoughts. "Caleb will be just fine." His commanding tone reassured her.

Raleigh's chest tightened with emotions. It had been so long since she'd had someone to lean on. She clutched Caleb to her and held on.

After what felt like an eternity, they roared into town, Dan skillfully steering the speeding pickup down the main thoroughfare and onward to the hospital.

Screeching to a stop outside the emergency doors, Dan threw the truck into park. "I'll be right back with some help," he said.

Raleigh watched him disappear through the door marked Emergency Entrance in red neon. She gently nudged her brother. "Caleb, honey, we're here."

Dan returned in record time, with a nurse pushing a wheelchair. He wrenched open the passenger-side door and together they helped Caleb from the pickup.

Doubling over, Caleb grasped his lower abdomen and groaned. The sound sent chills of horror pulsing down

Raleigh's spine. Only Dan's comforting arm wrapped securely around her shoulders kept her from collapsing in despair.

The nurse eased Caleb down into the wheelchair and whisked him inside.

"I'm going to move the truck to the visitor parking lot," Dan told her. "I'll be right back. Will you be okay?"

Raleigh nodded silently, took a deep breath and hurried to catch up with the nurse and Caleb.

The nurse took Caleb behind swinging double doors that announced Patients And Staff Only. Ignoring the sign, Raleigh pushed through the doors to find herself stopped by a tall man in a security officer's uniform. Around her, the emergency room writhed with activity.

Doctors and nurses scurried to and fro. The smell of antiseptic, blood and soap clung pervasively to the sterile white walls. Stainless-steel equipment glistened beneath the powerful lights. She heard buzzes, beeps, the strangled cry of frantic voices.

Ugly memories assailed her—memories of the other awful times she'd spent at the same hospital with Pa. Dizziness, nausea washed over her in waves.

"Miss?" The security officer addressed her.

Raleigh frowned at him. "Where's my brother?"

"I'm sorry, miss, you'll have to wait outside." Firmly, he grasped her elbow and directed her toward the door.

"But you don't understand," Raleigh protested. "He's the only family I've got left!" Her voice rose, high and shrill. Panic gnashed at her. They couldn't throw her out. They just couldn't. Caleb needed her.

The security guard's tone grew kind. "I know you're upset, but I guarantee they'll take good care of your brother. There's a waiting room around the corner, and as soon as the doctors know something, they'll come talk to you."

Raleigh toyed with an errant strand of hair sweeping down her neck, and plucked out a piece of straw. What else could she do?

Resigned, she allowed the security officer to lead her to the waiting room. Knotting her hands into fists to keep them from trembling, she plopped down on a worn vinyl bench, leaned her head against the wall, and wished for Dan.

Narrowing her eyes to slits, she stared with disinterest at the television mounted on the wall. Some late-night talk show host razzed a famous movie star. Raleigh sighed and tried not to think.

Crossing her legs, then immediately uncrossing them again, she opened her eyes and picked up a dog-eared magazine lying on the cheap wooden coffee table that bore cigarette burns and suspicious dark stains. The stains reminded her of blood, and she shivered.

Hospitals and their collection of wounded patients made Raleigh nervous. Focusing her eyes on the page before her, she tried to shut out the world around her.

"How is he?"

Raleigh looked up to see Dan. Relief flooded her.

"I don't know," she answered him.

Removing his hat, he sat down next to her. His stamina imbued her with strength, his mere presence braced her courage. "You holding up?"

"Yeah."

"Miss Travers?"

Raleigh turned to see a young man in a white lab coat, a black stethoscope dangling from his neck. She blinked. "Yes?"

"Hi, I'm Dr. Gilford." He extended his hand.

Raleigh shot to her feet. The magazine fluttered from her lap and slid to the floor with a soft slithering sound. She clasped the doctor's hand. "How is my brother?"

"I'm afraid we're going to have to take him in for an emergency appendectomy."

"Now? Tonight?"

"Yes. Time is of the essence. We want to get to him before the appendix ruptures. But don't worry, the procedure is very safe. We perform dozens each week."

Don't worry. Placating words. Easy for the doctor to say, it wasn't his brother. Soundlessly she nodded. They'd once told her not to worry about Pa, too.

Dr. Gilford smiled kindly. "It shouldn't take more than a couple of hours. The nurses are preparing him for surgery as we speak. Are you his legal guardian?"

"Yes."

"You'll have to register your brother and we'll need you to sign these consent forms." He extended a clipboard toward her. "And, by the way, do you have health insurance?"

"No." She took the clipboard and quickly perused the extensive sheet before signing it at the bottom.

"You'll have to go to the business office and make arrangements for payment, then," Dr. Gilford said.

"I'm paying the bill," Dan asserted.

"Well, that's fine, just stop by the admitting desk."

"And where would that be?" Dan asked.

"Wait," Raleigh interrupted. "I can't let you pay for Caleb's bill."

"We'll argue about this later," Dan said firmly. "I'll be back in a few minutes."

Following the doctor's directions, Dan disappeared around the corner. Raleigh was supremely glad to have Dan here, but at the same time she longed to deny that emotion. She could handle this on her own. Caleb was her brother. She didn't need Dan's help. Didn't need anybody except Caleb.

"When can I see my brother?" she asked Dr. Gilford.

"In a few minutes. They'll wheel him by on the way to O.R." He gave Raleigh an encouraging smile, then was gone, swallowed up by the imposing double doors separating her from Caleb.

Clasping her hands together, Raleigh sat back down, grew restless, stood up and paced. An elderly woman sitting across the room smiled at her. Raleigh shook her head, unable to smile back.

The doors swung open again and a stretcher popped through. Caleb lay on it, looking pale and frightened. The sight stabbed at her heart. Springing to his side, Raleigh grasped her brother's hand as the nurse and an orderly pushed him down the hall.

"How you doing, honey?"

"Okay," he whispered. His lips were cracked and dry.

"You'll be fine," Raleigh reassured him. She wanted to cry, to throw her head back and howl, but she knew from past experiences with death that the tears would not come. She'd been unable to cry for either of her parents or Jack. If only she could have cried, maybe then she would have felt cleansed, healed. But nature had denied her even that small release.

"Everything'll be all right, Raleigh," Caleb said, trying to comfort her. "I'm not going to die."

"Excuse me, miss," said the nurse. "You can wait right over there." She pointed to another waiting area in the alcove next to the operating room.

And then Caleb was gone, trundled through a similar set of double doors and out of Raleigh's sight.

Alone.

How empty the word sounded, how awful it felt. Alone, she sat down in the waiting room, stared at the pale beige wall, and steeled herself against the avalanche of feelings spinning inside her. First, she felt guilt, then anxiety, then an overwhelming melancholy, and finally, her old stand-by, anger.

She was mad at herself for having left Caleb to go on the hayride and she was mad at Daniel McClintock for coaxing her into it. Anger. An emotion more easily expressible than grief. She might not know how to cry, but she sure as heck knew how to get mad. Jumping to her feet, Raleigh viciously kicked a nearby chair.

"Hey, what's going on here?"

Raleigh jerked her head up and found herself staring at Daniel McClintock.

The cause of all her problems.

He held his cowboy hat in his hands, worrying the brim with his fingers. "I made the arrangements for Caleb's hospital bill."

"I'll pay you back every penny," she vowed.

"You don't owe me anything," Dan interrupted. "Your ideas for the ranch will make enough money to cover the costs, and I set up monthly installments. So, I don't want to hear any more about it."

"Caleb and I don't take handouts," she snapped, desperate to hide the pain and sorrow welling up inside her. She couldn't let Dan discover the truth about her.

"Simmer down," Dan said. "Everything's going to be all right."

"Ha," she barked bitterly. No way could Dan empathize with the utter terror she felt at the thought of losing her little brother. He wouldn't understand about Jack or why she believed herself jinxed—especially when it concerned her love life.

"I care, Raleigh. Why are you so afraid to let anyone get close to you?"

Why? Because, except for Caleb, everyone she'd ever loved had died tragically. She could not allow herself to care for Dan and bring destruction upon his head.

She folded her arms across her chest, felt her anger dissipate as she looked into Dan's concerned eyes. He'd shown her nothing but kindness and she had repaid him with the sharp edge of her temper. Chagrined, Raleigh dropped her gaze. Dan deserved better.

"Let's sit down." He inclined his head toward the bench. "I want to talk to you."

She settled into the seat and he eased down beside her. Laying his hat on the empty spot next to them, he steepled his fingers. "Do you know what I said to myself the minute I first saw you?"

"No."

"I thought, now here's a woman who could help me make my dreams come true."

"Did you?"

"Yes, I did. I recognized your strengths. You're one hell of a woman, Raleigh, but why do you fight so hard to hide your weaknesses? Everybody needs help sometimes."

"I don't."

"Who are you lying to, me or yourself?"

Raleigh stared down at her dusty boots, her wrinkled gingham dress. He was right. She longed to lean on him, to relinquish control and let him soothe her aching sorrow, but she didn't dare risk the luxury of his sheltering arms.

"Stop running away, and talk to me," Dan insisted.

"I've never run away from anything in my life!"

"You're kidding yourself. You might not run from hard work or responsibility, but you sure as hell run from personal involvement with people."

"People only hurt you in the end, why take the chance?" she said.

"May I sit here and wait with you? Be your friend? I care about Caleb, too."

His question took her by surprise. She hadn't expected him to settle for friendship.

"I don't know," she told him truthfully. Even friends caused pain.

She almost told him to leave, but the truth of the matter was, she wanted him to stay. Passing time alone in the forlorn waiting room, anticipating bad news, held little appeal.

"All right," she agreed.

"Thank you," he said simply, and leaned back against the wall.

They lapsed into an awkward silence, Raleigh acutely aware of his masculine presence. She couldn't stop thinking about their encounter in the back of the trailer. How long had it been since a man had shown an interest in her as a woman? More to the point, how long had it been since any man had been willing to chip past her mounted defenses and really get to know her?

Shifting his weight, Dan restlessly cracked his knuckles.

"You sure do that a lot," she commented.

"What?"

"Crack your knuckles."

"Oh." He shook his fingers. "Sorry, bad habit." Dan looked down at his hands and didn't say anything else. Raleigh turned her face away and studied the clock on the wall. Four-fifteen. She'd been up since before dawn and her body was feeling the effects of emotional stress and long hours. Her feet ached. Her eyes itched. Her muscles knotted. She blinked and yawned.

"How about I go find us a cup of coffee?" Dan asked.

"Sounds good," she said.

"You take it black, right?"

"Yes."

"See." He smiled. "I remember everything about you."

The second he was gone, a strange emptiness settled over her, as if the sunlight had been drained from the universe.

Dan wandered down the winding corridors searching for the cafeteria. He couldn't stop thinking about Raleigh and the events of last night, from the party to the hayride, to the very intense session they'd shared in the back of the tractor-trailer rig.

The memory stirred him. What would have happened if Caleb hadn't gotten sick? Would he and Raleigh have consummated their lurking passion? Would he have finally ruptured her bastion of defenses and unearthed her buried emotions? He didn't know.

After many false turns, Dan finally found several vending machines. He fed quarters into the slots, listening to them clink as they fell. He pushed buttons and waited for the paper cups to fill with wicked-looking coffee.

It didn't matter what might have happened between him and Raleigh. It was a moot point. Now they were back to where they'd started—Raleigh aloof and distant, pushing him away, erecting her angry barriers once more, keeping him at arm's length.

Dan sighed. He longed to hold her, comfort her, fortify her with his resilience. She desperately needed someone to lean on—he could see it clearly in her misty gray eyes—yet she didn't want his help. She resisted him. Resented him even.

Balancing the coffee cups, he ambled back down the corridor. What to do? Force the issue and maybe send her flying from the ranch? She teetered on the brink of surrendering to him. Dan had felt it in her famished kisses. But he also knew she perceived her body's needs as a weakness and that was the reason she'd reverted to her old angry stance. She hated to be dependent.

No, Dan decided. He couldn't force her to admit her true feelings for him. If he attempted to ensnare her, she'd disappear. So he would wait like a rock—quietly, solidly, eternally, whatever it took to win her trust. The next move belonged to Raleigh.

He returned with the coffee to find her sitting hunched over, her face buried in her hands. Her vulnerable posture stoked a poignant sense of sadness inside him. How he longed to protect her, to take care of her. If only she would let him into her heart.

At the sound of his footsteps, she lifted her head and gave him a tired, worn smile. "Thanks," she said, taking the cup he offered.

"Any news yet?" He inclined his head in the direction of the operating suite.

"No."

Another long hour passed. They sat side by side, fighting back yawns and watching the hands on the clock inch slowly forward.

It was five-thirty when Dr. Gilford came to speak to them, his green hospital scrubs blood splattered and his eyes red rimmed. The minute she spotted the doctor, Raleigh scrambled to her feet.

Dan rose beside her, resisting the urge to put his arm around her.

"How is he?" she squeaked.

"Your brother is doing just fine, Miss Travers. We'll be taking him to the recovery room in a few moments. You can visit him there."

"Thank you, doctor." She clasped the surgeon's hand. It hurt Dan to see her trembling. He wanted to soothe her, but if he tried, he knew she'd bristle like a porcupine.

"Caleb's going to be all right," she whispered to Dan as the doctor exited the area.

"Of course he is. Did you really doubt it?"

"Yes. I was terrified he wouldn't make it off the operating table alive."

"Oh, Raleigh, come here. You look like you could use a hug." He couldn't restrain himself any longer. He had to hold her. If she rejected him, then so be it. He held his arms wide and, to his surprise, she launched herself into his embrace.

Her head pressed into his chest felt so damned good, Dan could scarcely breathe. She rested there a moment, then quickly jerked back and stepped away.

"I need to see Caleb." She refused to meet his gaze.

"Let's go find the recovery room," he said, taking her hand, reluctant to relinquish contact with her. "It's got to be around here somewhere."

They walked down the silent corridor until they found the recovery room. Raleigh knocked on the door and a nurse answered. She led them to a small cubicle where Caleb lay sleeping.

"Five minutes only," the woman instructed, then left them alone.

Raleigh leaned over the stretcher and took her brother's hand. "Caleb? It's all over, honey. The surgery is finished. You came through with flying colors. It's me, Raleigh. I'm here."

Caleb's eyes fluttered open. "Am I suppose to feel better now?"

"Not for a while, I don't think." Reaching out, Raleigh gently ruffled his hair.

"That's good, 'cause it hurts like the dickens," he said, solemnly smoothing his hair back into place. Dan had witnessed that affectionate gesture between sister and brother a dozen times.

"I'll have the nurse bring you something for the pain," Raleigh promised.

"Hey, Dan." Caleb wriggled his fingers and Dan waved back.

"You better get well soon," Dan said. "We're planning another party for Halloween and we can't do it without you."

"You guys aren't mad at me, are you?"

"Why on earth would we be mad at you?" Raleigh asked.

"Because I spoiled your evening." Wincing, Caleb clutched his abdomen.

"Shh. You stop worrying about us." She leaned over and kissed his forehead. Dan shifted his weight. He felt uncomfortable, intruding on the tender family scene.

Caleb's eyelids, heavy from the effects of anesthesia, shuttered closed.

"We gotta go, honey. They're only letting us stay five minutes. But we'll be waiting outside."

The nurse arrived at the bedside with an injection for Caleb. "I'm sorry, you'll have to leave now," she said.

"See you later," Raleigh whispered.

Caleb nodded, too drowsy to speak.

Dan took Raleigh by the arm as they left the room. "Come on," he said. "I'm taking you out for breakfast and I refuse to take no for an answer."

* * *

Raleigh felt tired, cranky, and more than a little vulnerable. Her hair hung in shambles, her eyes ached, her stomach grumbled. More than anything, she wanted to be at her brother's bedside, holding his hand. Instead she found herself sitting in Dan's pickup, staring out the window at the brightening sky.

She'd been very grateful for his company during Caleb's surgery. His calm, quiet manner soothed her like a balm, but it also scared her. She could not afford the luxury of liking Dan too much. She must keep her feelings hidden from him. She had to protect herself at all costs.

"You okay?" he asked, slipping the truck into gear and turning out of the hospital parking lot.

"Yeah."

"You can cry if you want. I'll understand. Might make you feel better."

Violently she shook her head, disheveled hair tumbling around her shoulders. She pressed her palms to her burning eyelids. She'd love a good cry, but she knew from experience that the tears would not come.

"You've been through a great deal in the last twenty-four hours," Dan said.

"Yeah," she agreed, her voice cracking.

"Where would you like to go for breakfast?"

Raleigh sighed. "I'm not up to tackling a restaurant. Besides, I don't feel right leaving Caleb all alone."

"The nurse gave him a shot. He'll sleep for hours. Relax, Raleigh, they'll take good care of him."

"I suppose you're right," she mumbled, unable to shake the nagging guilt.

"Easy now." Dan spoke as if talking to a skittish horse. "Why don't we just go back to the ranch? You can take a shower while I make breakfast. Maybe I can even persuade you to take a nap."

His plan made sense. She was tired, rumpled and hungry. "Okay," she agreed. "For a little while."

Dan turned the pickup in the direction of Clyde. Raleigh had almost nodded off by the time Dan pulled into the driveway.

They trudged into the log cabin, not wanting to disturb Pete asleep in the big house. Raleigh went to shower while Dan rustled up breakfast.

Several minutes later she sat down at the kitchen table, wrapped in a terry-cloth bathrobe, the smell of bacon and eggs filtering throughout the small cabin.

"I thought you might want to talk," Dan said, sliding a plate in front of her.

"What for?"

He settled in across from her with a plate of his own. "It might help to express your feelings."

"I'm scared," she said before she even knew what she was going to say. Why was she telling him this? Hadn't she always kept her problems a closely guarded secret? She feared opening up to him more than anything. Revealing her true feelings made her too vulnerable to pain.

"Of what?" Dan asked, his chocolate brown eyes prying and curious.

"Losing Caleb."

"Why?"

"He could have died tonight."

"Not very likely."

"I don't know what I'd do if anything happened to him." She swallowed hard, the thought too terrifying to entertain. "Have you ever lost someone you love?"

"No, not by death." Dan sipped his coffee and waited for her to continue.

"Then you can't know what it's like."

"I know what it's like to have a broken heart."

"It's not the same thing." She shuddered. "Not at all."

"You hold on to Caleb too tightly. You've got to let him grow up, Raleigh."

"How can I let him go? He's all I've got."

"You could have me," Dan said softly.

Raleigh glared at Dan. Was her panic reflected on her face? "I've tried to tell you again and again, I'm not looking for a man. I don't want to fall in love. Don't you get it?"

"No."

"There is no such thing as happily-ever-after. It's a myth. A fairy tale for children."

"What did he do to you?" Dan asked harshly.

"Who?"

"The man who broke your heart."

Raleigh glanced down at her untouched plate, trying to escape Dan's penetrating stare. "You don't understand," she whispered.

He reached across the table and took her hand. "I'd like to know. Please. I want to help heal the wounds."

"No," she rasped. "It's not possible." She couldn't allow him to know her tragedies, then he would pity her, and she couldn't stand that.

"Share," he insisted, his thumb rubbing her palm until tingles rushed up her arm.

"I can't!"

"I'm not letting you off the hook. You've kept things hidden too long. Talking about it is the *only* way you're going to get over it."

She kept staring at her plate.

"Look at me, Raleigh. I have to know why you won't let yourself be loved. You owe me that much of an explanation."

Slowly she raised her eyes, met his, and saw confusion written on his dear face. It would be so easy to let herself care for him. Too easy.

"Maybe this has nothing to do with my past, Dan. Maybe I just don't like you."

"Nice try, darling, but I'm not buying it. When we kiss, I feel something potent, and I know you feel it, too. That's why you're fighting so hard. Wouldn't you like to exorcise the ghosts that haunt you? Wouldn't you like to be free to love again?"

"If I tell you, will you stop badgering me?"

He held up three fingers. "Scout's honor."

She sighed, then spoke in a rush. "My mother died when I was ten. My fiancé died when I was eighteen. My pa died last year. I'm tired of everybody I love dying, so I figure I won't love anybody else. End of story."

"Whoa, slow down."

Rolling her eyes, she crunched a piece of bacon between her teeth. "I knew you wouldn't quit bugging me."

"How did your mother die?"

"In a house fire." She'd said the words as fast as she could, hoping she wouldn't feel the gut-wrenching impact. But it did no good. Guilt, heavy as a goose-down quilt, enveloped her. She had taken eight-month-old Caleb to the park while her mother napped off a migraine. When they'd returned, she'd found their house engulfed in flames. Raleigh closed her eyes against the agonizing memories—the acrid smell of smoke, the screaming fire engine sirens, the stark terror she'd felt as she'd screamed for her mother.

Why hadn't she died in the fire, too? Everything would have been easier and she wouldn't have had to bear so much pain. Opening her eyes, she discovered Dan watching her intently. Maybe he was right. Maybe talking about it would help. Keeping silent certainly hadn't eased her suffering.

"It gets worse," she said. "Are you sure you want to hear this?"

"Yes," Dan said. "Tell me. What happened to your fiancé?"

Raleigh gulped against the resurging agony. "I caused Jack's death."

Chapter Nine

"**W**hat?" Dan clenched the edge of the table with both hands.

Once she started talking, Raleigh took a perverse sense of pleasure in telling him. He had goaded her into this. She would find out for sure if he really did want to share her burdens and nightmares.

"I practically killed Jack."

"How?"

She wadded up her paper napkin, then unfurled it. "When I was in high school, I fell in love with Jack Carter. He was so handsome, I couldn't believe he'd asked me out."

Dan leaned forward, all his attention trained on her.

"Jack was class president," she continued, "captain of the football team and a first-class swimmer. We spent every weekend that summer at Lake Brownwood. Jack was dedicated to swimming. He dreamed of going to the Olympics."

"So what went wrong?"

Raleigh twisted the napkin around her index finger and took a deep breath. "After graduation, we'd planned to get married. Jack had been offered a job working in the oil fields, but he wasn't satisfied. He wanted bigger and better things—fame, fortune. He was always talking about swimming. He vowed to win the gold and make millions from product endorsements." Raleigh stopped, the words freezing in her throat.

"Go on," Dan prompted.

"We were alone at the lake one Saturday night. Jack had had a couple of beers." She took a deep breath, remembering.

It was past midnight. There was a full moon and the water shimmered inky black. She could still hear frogs croaking, still smell honeysuckle choking the night air. They had spread a blanket on the shore and Jack had been talking about the Olympics again.

"He wanted to impress me with a new swimming technique he'd developed. He kept talking about it. He wanted to show me it right then."

As she spoke the words Raleigh felt strangely detached, as if the events she related had happened to someone else. She stared down at her hand and released her death grip on the napkin.

"I tried to get him to wait until morning to demonstrate his new skill, but Jack was insistent." Taking a sip of her now-cold coffee, she looked at Dan. He sat as if hypnotized, waiting for her to continue.

"Lake Brownwood is treacherous. Lots of tree stumps and undercurrents. Even in daylight, it's dangerous to swim there."

Dan nodded, folding his hands into fists, the color draining from his face.

"I tried to talk him out of it," she whispered. "But Jack loved to show off."

"You poor kid."

"I told him he didn't have anything to prove to me. He had been drinking, after all, and I was worried. He called me a 'fraidy cat', kissed me, stripped off his shirt, and dived in."

Dan hissed.

"I stood on the bank watching him in the moonlight. He looked so graceful, so perfect . . ." Raleigh hesitated.

"Raleigh?"

"I'm okay," she said at last, lifting a hand to her throat and swallowing hard.

"You don't have to say any more."

"No. You're right. I haven't spoken about it since that day. I need to get it out." Her voice echoed in her own ears, hard, cold, dead.

"But you didn't kill him," Dan argued.

"Not directly, no. But I was responsible. See, I can't swim, at least not very well. Jack was halfway across the lake when he suddenly disappeared." The memory that had haunted her for years made her want to sob—but she never cried.

"At first I thought he was teasing me," she continued. "Horsing around. I waited one minute. Two. Three. Then I panicked."

"I can't imagine what you went through," Dan said, his voice soft with sympathy.

"I screamed for him. There wasn't even a ripple on the water." She shuddered. Her eyes felt as raw as if they'd been rubbed with sandpaper. Even at the time, she'd been unable to mourn for Jack with proper tears. "I splashed in waist-deep, but I was too scared to go farther. I knew I would drown, too, if I tried to save him."

"And you were only eighteen?"

She nodded. "His parents found me sitting on the bank at dawn. I was rocking back and forth and babbling about Jack and the Olympics."

"It wasn't your fault, Raleigh." Dan patted her hand, his touch soothing her more than she ever thought possible.

"Jack's parents blamed me. They said I was responsible. If he hadn't been out with me in the first place, it wouldn't have happened. I let their son go in. I didn't stop him. I didn't run for help. I just sat there like an idiot waiting for him to come back."

"You were just a kid. You were in shock. How dare they blame you." Dan smacked his fist into his palm.

"Jack was their only child. They needed to assuage their own grief, so they lashed out at me. I realize that now, but at the time I believed them." Her bottom lip trembled.

"Damn, Raleigh, how on earth did you survive?"

"Pa and Caleb pulled me through it. I had nightmares for months. But then Pa made me his partner, got me focused on doing something I loved. Shoeing horses was my therapy, my salvation."

"I've never known anyone who had to face such terrible catastrophes at such a young age." Dan clicked his tongue in sympathy.

"It wasn't long after Jack's death that we found out Pa had kidney failure. His illness really took a toll on me. I was the one who drove him to dialysis in Abilene three times a week, and I practically took over the business when he became too weak to work."

"Life has sure thrown you some curveballs."

"Oh, Dan, it's not just fate."

"What do you mean?"

"It's me. I'm the jinx."

"Raleigh, you can't blame yourself. These things happen. It's unfortunate, but nothing was your fault." His fingers curled around her arm.

"I'm a black widow. Anybody who loves me dies."

"Caleb didn't die."

"So far," Raleigh said bitterly. "I live with the constant fear of losing him." She twisted from his grasp.

"You're being irrational."

"Am I? Sorry, Dan, I can't risk that conclusion. I can't afford to fall in love again. My heart just couldn't take it."

"That's nonsense, Raleigh. You've already suffered so much, you're due for good times." He tried to reach for her again, but she moved aside.

"Is it nonsense, Dan? Do you still want a relationship with me? Because if you do, I'm warning you right now, you're taking your life in your hands."

Her anguish caused him physical pain. Dan absorbed her tragic story, felt the effects twist his gut as if he'd consumed a thousand chili peppers. When he considered all she'd suffered, he literally ached for her.

More than anything, he wanted to ease her sorrow. He longed to take her into his arms, hold her safe and secure for the rest of their lives.

"Raleigh, please let me help."

She jumped up and started clearing the dishes off the table without answering him.

Dan stared down at his hands. How to reach her? How to let her know he wanted to love her no matter what the risks, real or imagined?

She believed she was a jinx and he could see where she might have assumed that crazy notion. He needed to convince Raleigh to trust him, to free herself from guilt's restrictive shackles.

Dan resisted the urge to shake some sense into her, to tell her he loved her. He knew he must proceed with extreme caution if he ever hoped to capture Raleigh's heart.

"Will you take me back to the hospital now? I've been away from Caleb too long," she asked when she'd finished washing the breakfast dishes. Her gray eyes were red rimmed and she looked beat to a frazzle. She held her shoulders ramrod straight, as if she bore the weight of the world on her fragile frame.

"No," he said firmly. "You need to take a nap first."

"Fine," she snapped. "I'll drive myself."

He pulled the keys from his pocket and dangled them in front of her. "I've got the keys."

"Then I'll drive my truck."

"I don't want you on the highway in that rattle-trap heap."

"Well, it's not your decision to make, is it?" She sank her hands on her hips and flashed him a look of warning.

Even exhausted and defiant, she was beautiful. He admired her resilience, her sense of responsibility, her fierce independence. Yet those were the very same qualities that separated them. Winning Raleigh's love might prove to be the biggest challenge of his life. But Daniel J. McClintock never backed down from a challenge.

"Let's compromise. I'll call the hospital and check on Caleb, and we'll both take a two-hour nap. Then I promise to drive you back to Abilene. You can't help your brother if you're on the verge of collapse."

"I can sleep on the floor in his room."

"Damn it, Raleigh, be sensible."

"He's my brother, my responsibility. Caleb's not your problem, Dan, so get out of my way."

Her exasperating manner goaded him to throw caution to the wind. He had to make her understand. "Don't you get it, Raleigh? I want to make your problems my problems.''

She put her hands over her ears. "Stop it, Dan. I don't want to hear this."

He tugged her hands from her ears. "Well, you're going to listen to me, because what I have to say will affect both of us for the rest of our lives."

"No," she whimpered. "Please don't say it." She couldn't bear it if he articulated the very words she dreaded hearing more than any other in the English language.

Fire blazed in his dark eyes. A corresponding rush coursed through her veins. Tension screwed the corners of his mouth into a tight grimace. "Raleigh, you're tired and upset. We can talk about this later and work everything out."

"No, we can't." Distressed, she hopped from foot to foot. "Now I have to move and find another job."

"For heaven's sake, why?"

"I can't stay here," she said, a heavy sensation of claustrophobia settling over her. She felt trapped, cornered. If she stayed, she feared Dan would confess his love for her and she simply could not deal with that declaration.

"I still don't understand why you feel you have to leave." He inclined his head.

"I told you, I'm a jinx, bad luck."

"I promise not to hurt you."

"Don't you get it? "I'd be the one hurting you. I destroyed my whole family with their love for me."

"That's ridiculous thinking."

"I can't risk it."

"You're a hardheaded little billy goat."

"Good. Stubbornness is the only thing that protects me," she declared.

He reached for her, but she shied, almost stumbling in her haste to get away.

"Don't touch me, Dan."

For years she'd held back her feelings, denied most emotions except anger. One way or another, she had to convince him to leave her alone. She was deathly afraid she wanted him, too. What if she surrendered to the feeling and allowed herself to love him?

She shuddered, imagining Dan being killed. Would he be kicked by a horse? Ground under the wheels of some machinery? Or maybe something as innocuous as pneumonia? Raleigh knew she couldn't survive the demise of another loved one. Already she'd been so abused by life, she couldn't cry, couldn't care. How could she knowingly ask for more sorrow?

"Raleigh? Answer me," Dan insisted. "I've got to know. Why won't you put the past to rest?"

She had to do something, had to get rid of him before she lost control and threw herself into his welcoming arms. To save herself, to save Dan, Raleigh told the biggest lie of her life.

"Because," she cried, "I could never love you!"

Shocked, Dan stared at her wide-eyed. His body jerked as if controlled by marionette strings. He plucked his cowboy hat off the kitchen table and squeezed it between his fingers.

He felt used, dirty, betrayed by his own heart. Just when he'd been about to reveal his true feelings to her, Raleigh had effectively shot him down. Thank God, he hadn't been fool enough to utter the word *love*.

She ducked her head, obviously uncomfortable with his dismay. "Caleb and I will be leaving the ranch, of course. We can't stay here under the circumstances," she mumbled, turning her back on him.

Dan's mouth dropped open. Her vehement denial attacked him without warning, ambushing him out of nowhere. He'd been so completely wrong. Had someone smashed him in the head with a two-by-four? Had the world stopped spinning? Here he'd been thinking she just needed a little time, some space and reassurance. He hadn't realized she could never love him in return.

Numbed by the stunning implications of her cruel words, he felt dead inside. How could he have been so blind?

"Where will you go?" he asked dully.

"That's really none of your concern, is it?"

Mentally kicking himself, Dan spun on his heel and left her standing there, desperate to escape and hide his anguish. Pain, sharp and unrelenting, pelted him.

Dan slammed the cabin door without looking back. A dark sucking chest wound had taken the place of his heart. A knife in his sternum would have been kinder and scarred much less than Raleigh's hateful statement.

He stalked across the exercise yard, kicking aside litter and debris left from last night's party. Had it only been a few short hours since he'd held Raleigh in his arms in the back of the trailer? Dan winced. Nothing had ever hurt like this. Even when Jenny Harris had abandoned him at the altar in front of friends and family, he hadn't felt this empty.

Was he doomed to keep loving women who couldn't love him in return? Because Raleigh made him feel so alive, so stimulated, so happy, he assumed she'd felt the same for him. What a mistake.

He should have listened to his father and remained in Dallas. What was the point of chasing after his dream if Raleigh wasn't around to share it with him? No. Dan shook his head. That was regressive thinking. The old man's derisive laughter resounded in his ears. Despite the problems in his personal life, he refused to tuck his tail between his legs and run home to Daddy.

He stalked into the big house in time to hear the phone ring. Snatching up the receiver, he barked a curt hello.

"Why, good morning to you, too, son."

Dan cringed. As usual, his father's timing was lousy.

"Did I catch you at a bad time?" his father asked.

Dan sank into a chair and ran his fingers through his hair. "What do you want?"

"Fine way to talk to your father."

"Sorry, Dad, I've got a lot on my mind."

"I thought you might want to know your mother and I are going to be in Abilene next week on business. We'd like to drop by and check out this little ranch of yours. That okay by you?"

Dan held his tongue. His father was putting him down again. What else had he expected? He should have gotten used to it by now.

"Sure, Dad. Come on down." He had nothing to hide. He was proud of his ranch and the work they'd accomplished.

"Now, we don't want to inconvenience you, son. You don't want us there, you just say so. I mean, if your place isn't up to snuff."

Dan resented the typical dig at his competence. Bristling, he got to his feet. He was not about to let his father push him around anymore. Time to take a stand. Raleigh might have broken his heart but she hadn't destroyed his courage. He was a survivor. He would manage somehow.

"You be here, Dad. I'll be damn proud to show you my place."

"We'll be arriving next Friday. That suit you?" Bill McClintock sounded slightly taken aback.

Dan grinned, suddenly feeling invincible. "Yeah, Dad. I'll be looking forward to your visit."

What had she done?

Raleigh had thought it would be easier to make Dan believe she didn't care about him. Instead she'd made things far worse. She should have told him the truth, admitted that she was afraid, that she needed more time. But he had rushed her, demanding the kind of commitment she didn't know if she would ever be able to give.

Too late, the hideous words had flown out of her mouth, gashing deep ugly scars on his heart, and she didn't know how to repair the wounds.

But she had to admit to herself that although it might be painful for Dan now, it was for the best in the long run. She had to end the relationship before it went any further, and that meant leaving the ranch as quickly as possible.

While her resolve simmered strong, she picked up the phone and dialed Fay Walton's number. Sucking in a deep breath, she wrapped the telephone cord around her fingers.

"Hello?"

"Fay?"

"Raleigh? Kitten, is that you?"

"Uh-huh," she replied, her voice tremulous.

"What's wrong?"

"Caleb's in the hospital, and Dan and I have split ways, so I've got to find someplace else for us to live."

"What happened to Caleb?" Fay asked, alarmed.

Raleigh filled her in on both Caleb's surgery and the fiasco with Dan.

"I'm so sorry about Caleb. I wish I'd known. I never would have left him alone last night, but he told me he felt fine."

"It's not your fault," Raleigh assured her. "The doctor said he'll be okay."

"How are you holding up?"

"Been better."

"Too bad things didn't work out with you and Dan," Fay sympathized. "I really believed you two might have something going."

"I've got to get away from here."

"Pack up your things and get on over to my place, you hear me? You can help me out at the diner again until you find something else."

"Oh, Fay, you're the best friend in the entire world."

"Everything will work out just fine, kitten. Don't give up. Trust me."

Before her brother was released from the hospital, Pete helped Raleigh move her and Caleb's meager belongings to Fay's small house on the outskirts of Clyde.

Prudently, Dan stayed away during the move. Raleigh hated to inconvenience Fay, but the idea of staying at the ranch even one day longer than necessary motivated her to leave immediately.

But despite her best efforts to erase him from her memory, Daniel McClintock haunted her thoughts. Determined to steel herself, Raleigh clamped down on her emotions like a bulldog gnawing a rag. After years of denying her true feelings, she found it surprisingly easy to numb herself. She refused to let herself care.

By Friday, five days after she'd left the ranch, Raleigh was a nervous wreck. Her appetite vanished and she knew without weighing herself that she'd lost several pounds, but no food enticed her. She had trouble sleeping on Fay's narrow sofa, waking frequently in the night to stare at the wall, trying to dispel the images of Daniel McClintock clogging her brain.

Before going to work at the diner, Raleigh had stationed Caleb on the couch in Fay's living room, remote control in his hand and snacks on the nearby tray. He'd been released from the hospital the day before and although he still looked ill, he was healing. Her brother had asked about Dan but Raleigh simply told him they would never be returning to the ranch, then she'd hurried out the door before he could demand to know the reason why.

"There's one hell of a sandstorm brewing. You can see it hovering on the horizon. Radio says it's coming in from New Mexico," Annie commented, shaking out a match in the ashtray.

"Yeah." Fay nodded. "I can smell it."

"We gonna close early if it hits?" Annie asked, lazily blowing smoke rings at the ceiling.

"Maybe," Fay hedged.

Raleigh caught herself wondering if Pete or Dan would remember to put the horses in the barn. The sandstorm would make them unruly. They could injure themselves. She worried. It upset her to think the horses might not be getting the kind of care they deserved.

Annie pushed back her chair. "I'm going for a cup of java. Anybody else want one?"

"None for me, thanks," Fay said.

"Raleigh?"

"Huh?" She jerked, blinked, looked at Fay.

"Annie's getting coffee, want some?"

"No."

"You were a thousand miles away. A penny for your thoughts," Fay commented once Annie had disappeared into the kitchen.

Shrugging, Raleigh propped her chin in her palm. "I'm worried about Dan's horses."

"You miss him, don't you?"

"I miss the horses."

Fay shook her head. "Raleigh, you don't have to put up a big front for me. I don't know what happened between you two, and it's really none of my business, but I think you're making a big mistake."

Raleigh narrowed her eyes. Was she really that transparent?

"Do you know why your father and I never got married?" Fay asked.

"Caleb and I always hoped you would."

"Believe you me, I wanted to marry Will Travers more than any man on the face of this earth. I loved your pa."

"He loved you, too," Raleigh said.

"No, kitten, I don't think he did. Not in the way he loved your mother. He couldn't get over her, Raleigh. He wouldn't let himself."

"Pa cared about you, I know he did."

"He never told *me* he loved me, and I badly needed to hear those words."

"Maybe he was just scared."

"Like I wasn't? No. He couldn't relinquish the past in order to live in the future."

Was it true? A spasm of grief rippled through Raleigh at the thought of her father's self-imposed unhappiness.

"I hate seeing you make the same mistakes your pa made," Fay continued, "and I know you're plumb miserable. You closed yourself off to love when Jack died. I know your father had a hand in that, too. Don't deny it. We fought over you. I heard him telling you that you didn't need a man to be complete. That's why he taught you to shoe horses, so you could be strong and independent. Although he meant well, your pa did you a great disservice."

"He was my father," Raleigh rasped, the truth of Fay's words cutting deeper than any physical suffering ever could. But her friend wasn't about to let up.

"Then Dan came along and tried to pry you out of your reclusive shell, and you turned your back on him. Just like your pa turned his back on me. It hurts to see history repeating itself." Fay sighed.

"I'm so afraid if I let myself love Dan, something awful will happen to him." Raleigh clasped her hands in her lap to keep them from shaking. "I'm terrified he'll end up like everyone else I've ever loved."

"You know something? Your father was so scared of falling in love with me, he wouldn't even spend the night." Fay gazed off into the distance, remembering. "He'd come visit awhile, then leave me with empty arms and a lonely bed. Damn it, Raleigh, he broke my heart."

Fay's voice cracked and tears glistened in her eyes. Clearing her throat, she sniffled and slashed at her eyes with the back of her hand. "But that's all past now."

"I had no idea." Raleigh stared at Fay. "You two seemed so happy together."

"That's the hell of it. We were happy." Fay fiddled with her apron strings. "I'm not telling you this to upset you, Raleigh, but it's important to understand. I want you to break the cycle. Don't forsake Dan. He obviously cares for you very much."

"Fay, I can't handle this relationship."

"How do you know unless you try?"

"It's too risky," Raleigh whispered.

Raleigh could see stark sorrow written on Fay's dear face. "Honey, if you let Dan slip away, I promise you, you'll regret it for the rest of your life."

Chapter Ten

Dan stopped unloading the truck and cast a wary eye toward the darkening sky. A bunker of brown clouds rolled steadily eastward. Unfortunate, he thought, that the storm had arrived too late to prevent his parents' incoming flight. Pete had already gone to Abilene to pick them up at the airport. Dan savored their visit like a root canal.

The last week without Raleigh had been pure hell. The horses, somehow sensing their mistress had left for good, misbehaved, refusing to cooperate with either him or Pete. Even Matt Dillon had nipped at him earlier in the afternoon. He couldn't blame the animals. Without Raleigh, he felt irritable, distracted, and downright ornery himself.

And now his parents were about to descend upon him in the middle of a sandstorm. What else could go wrong? he wondered, shouldering a fifty-pound sack of oats and heading for the barn.

Halfway across the yard he stopped dead in his tracks. The corral gate hung open, creaking with each billowing gust of dusty wind. All the horses were gone except for Matt Dillon and Sunny, who were enclosed in a separate paddock.

''Damn,'' Dan swore, dropping the oats to the ground. Obviously, either he or Pete had left the gate unlocked. This wouldn't have happened if Raleigh had been here, he thought, squinting into the distance.

No sign of the missing horses. Damn. He couldn't leave the animals out in a sandstorm, they might get hurt. There was no choice but to go after them. Dan looked at his watch and then at the sky. No time to wait for Pete, the situation was urgent. But where to start looking?

If only Raleigh were here, she'd know what to do. Dan shook his head. Useless thinking. This was his ranch, and he could handle a crisis.

Disgusted, he stalked to the barn, Chester hot on his heels. He grabbed his gear and quickly saddled Matt Dillon. Another glance at the ominous sky told Dan he had maybe an hour before the storm hit. Leading the gelding out of the paddock, he latched the gate, then swung into the saddle.

Galloping across the pasture, Dan followed the hoof-prints as best he could, Chester trotting behind him.

He rode for several minutes, the storm rolling in faster than he'd expected. Anxiety gripped his gut.

The wind kicked up, blowing sand and dirt into his face. Grit coated his lips. He spat and wiped his mouth with a blue bandanna he dug from his back pocket.

Each step took him deeper and deeper into the storm. In his mind, Raleigh rode beside him, fortifying his imagination with her undaunted courage. Even though she'd told him she didn't love him, Dan had trouble believing she was gone for good. He still felt her presence, in his heart, in his soul.

Hunkering in the saddle, he bunched his shoulders for protection against the growing wind, and coughed. Sand eddies danced and swirled before him. He tugged on the reins and turned Matt Dillon to the left.

He skirted a clump of cacti and traveled over a rocky ridge. His eyes burned. His nose itched. He rubbed his mouth with a knuckle, and tasted dirt.

Evil, dark clouds boiled above, threatening a sandy deluge. The encroaching gale whistled through the rocky canyon. He couldn't see two feet in front of his face, much less hoofprints in the shifting earth.

Chester shied, barking furiously. Dan urged Matt Dillon onward, but the gelding balked.

Dan drove his heels into the Thoroughbred's sides. "Come on, come on."

Matt Dillon snorted, thrashed his head.

Then Dan heard it, clear and unmistakable—a rattlesnake's deadly buzz.

Matt Dillon reared, bucked, kicked, fought the bit.

A violent snatch of wind grabbed Dan's hat and sent it flying across the rugged terrain. Grinding his teeth, Dan struggled to stay astride the frightened horse.

"Whoa, there. Whoa, boy."

The rattling grew louder, more insistent.

Dan scanned the ground, trying unsuccessfully to locate the snake and steer the horse clear.

Matt Dillon reared again, his hooves clattering against the rocks. The Thoroughbred tugged sharply on the bridle, seeking to rid himself of his passenger. The leather reins chewed Dan's palms as he fought desperately to remain in the saddle.

But this time Dan wasn't so lucky. His aching fingers slipped. He lost his balance and succumbed to the bucking animal's attempts to dislodge him. Arms and legs windmilling wildly, he snatched for a handful of Matt Dillon's mane and missed.

He cried out seconds before his head struck a large, flat rock and his thoughts fractured into silence.

Raleigh knew Fay was right. She loved Dan, wanted him, needed him, couldn't live without him. No matter how hard she struggled to deny it, he'd embedded himself in her psyche like a farrier's nail in a horseshoe.

They complemented each other—his calm nature soothed her fiery tendencies, while her down-to-earth practical approach to problem solving helped offset his dreaminess. Like a bit and bridle, they fit, wonderful as a team, ineffective alone.

She had to find Dan and tell him the truth. Now. Today. This minute. For at last she was ready to admit her love, both to Dan and herself. Finally she had a chance for happiness.

"Fay," Raleigh said, looking her dear friend straight in the eye. "I have to go to the ranch."

"In this storm?" Concern knit Fay's brow.

Raleigh got to her feet, removed her apron, and retrieved her purse from behind the counter. Fay followed her to the doorway, pushing up the sleeves of her sweater as she went. The wind seized the front door from her hand and smacked it against the outside wall with a resounding bang.

"Will you look after Caleb for me until I get back?" Raleigh had to shout over the wind to be heard.

"Of course I will. Good luck."

Raleigh waved goodbye and dashed down the block, her pink uniform flapping around her legs in the thick, dusty breeze.

At the thought of seeing Dan again, excitement and dread mixed inside her like an exotic cocktail. She gunned the engine and maneuvered her battered old pickup through the gathering storm.

Fists of sand splattered against the windshield. She turned on the wipers, but they only smeared the dirt, decreasing her visibility even more.

When she finally reached the ranch it was only to find it empty. Dan's truck sat in the driveway, keys swinging from the ignition. The corral gate hung open and there were no horses in sight. Had the animals gotten out of their enclosure? Raleigh worried. In this storm?

"Dan," she called, cupping her hands around her mouth. The wind slapped the echo back in her face.

Blowing sand filled her sneakered feet. The wind roared steadily. Squinting against the dust, she saw Sunny silhouetted in the paddock.

Then, she heard the faint sound of barking. From out of the dust clouds ran Chester, tongue lolling.

"Hey, Chester," she greeted him.

The dog whined.

"What's the matter, boy? You hungry? Hasn't Dan been feeding you since I left?"

Chester whined louder, pawing at her leg. He barked sharply and turned in a semicircle, as if trying to tell her something.

"What is it, boy?"

Growling, Chester hunkered down on the ground and laid back his ears.

A disturbing intuitive flash told Raleigh something was very wrong, that Dan was in trouble. She certainly couldn't stand by and do nothing while the man she loved was in danger. She'd fallen prey to that tragic mistake once and she wasn't about to do it again.

Unlatching the paddock, she led Sunny outside, ignoring the increasing tempo of the storm. Not bothering with a saddle, she swung onto the mare's back and started across the pasture, Chester leading the way.

Savage blasts of sand impeded her progress. She could scarcely see. If it hadn't been for the dog, she wouldn't have known which direction to go.

Stark images dominated her mind's eye. Her mother's fiery death. Jack's pale, lifeless body wrenched from the murky waters by rescue workers. Pa, weak and frail, being wheeled into surgery for the kidney transplant that had ended his life.

And Dan. The way he had looked the last time she'd spoken those cutting, lying words. She'd caused him so much pain. What a fool she'd been. Life was so short. Too short. Letting her pride and fears get in the way of life, allowing her anger and shame to get in the way of love. Now that she realized the error of her actions, it might be too late to change, too late to undo her hateful statement.

Too late to tell Dan she loved him.

For the first time in many years, she teetered on the brink of tears. A river of sorrow pressed against her eyelids, threatening to break through the levee of her loneliness and come cascading down her cheeks in unstoppable torrents.

The wind howled, cold and desolate.

Sand clung to her eyelashes, her nose, her mouth. Sneezing, she squinted into the darkness, trying to decipher Chester's skulking shape ambling just ahead of her. Everywhere she looked she saw whirlwinds of dust, debris and sand snuffing out the last shreds of daylight.

To her left, she heard Chester bark. She tried to turn Sunny west, into the wind, but the mare tossed her head and stepped gingerly through the sand, obviously reluctant to move.

Raleigh sank her heels into the horse's flanks. "Come on, Sunny, you can do it."

Then, out of the blackness, Matt Dillon emerged, galloping for his life, dragging Dan's saddle behind him. Raleigh caught a fleeting glimpse of the terrified Thoroughbred as he thundered away.

Oh, no, she fretted, Dan had been thrown. He was out there somewhere in the sandstorm, alone, possibly injured. Fear tightened her throat as a barrage of awful possibilities assaulted her mind.

Raleigh stifled a moan of despair. She had to remain calm.

Leaning over Sunny, she continued to urge the mare forward, following Chester's steady barking. If it weren't for the dog, she'd be totally adrift in a sea of blinding sand. She tugged her sweater more tightly around her shoulders, but it provided precious little protection against the mounting cold, and none whatsoever against the accumulating grit.

"Oh, Dan, where are you?" she whispered. "What's happened?"

It seemed hours passed, although she knew it was only a matter of minutes. In this seething black pit of sand-filled hell, reality became fantasy and fantasy, reality. She even lost her sense of direction.

Doubt clouded her thoughts. Maybe Chester didn't know where Dan was. Maybe this was a wild-goose chase. For all she knew, she might be headed straight back to the ranch.

Chester's barking grew louder as she approached. Her stomach twisted. Something was very wrong.

She slipped off Sunny's back, but held tightly to the reins, avoiding the risk of the mare taking flight. Extending her right hand in front of her, she stumbled forward, searching like a blind woman, her fingers grasping for landmarks.

"Chester," she shouted.

The dog yipped excitedly.

Dear God, she prayed. Please let Dan be all right.

She tripped over a rock and fell to her knees. Brushing sand from her eyes, she stared at what lay directly in front of her.

An unmoving form sprawled across a rocky ridge. She knew instantly it was Dan.

Her heart pounded, injecting her with a fresh jolt of energy. Staggering to her feet, she struggled toward Dan, ignoring the thorns and grass burrs pricking her knees and palms.

She scaled the small ridge, pulling herself up beside him, all the while clinging to Sunny's reins. She reached for Dan, fingers trembling.

"Dan?" Her voice cracked.

No response.

She tasted terror, grim and metallic. Touching him, she found he felt cold. So very cold.

Inching closer, she squatted over him, her knees tucked under her chin. She laid her cheek against his face but experienced no warm breath on her skin. In the darkness she couldn't see his chest rise and fall. She grappled for a pulse at his wrist, but felt no reassuring thud.

She grabbed him by the shoulders and gently shook him. His head rolled limply. She saw a small pool of dark blood staining the ground beneath him.

"Dan!" she screamed, and for one hideous moment, thought he was dead.

* * *

He heard her calling to him through the mist. Raleigh. His girl. How had she gotten so far away?

Struggling through the boggy swamp of his mind, he willed his eyes to open, his mouth to speak, but he felt so heavy, weighted, leaden, lost in a forest of blackness.

Her fingers gripped his. Where was he? What had happened?

Oh, yes. He remembered. The horses, the storm, his parents were coming. But why was Raleigh here and how had he hurt his head? Groaning, he raised a hand to the painful knot at his temple, felt something wet and sticky. Blood?

He heard a sob. Raleigh? Crying?

"Oh, Dan, you're alive, you're alive!"

Prying his eyes open, he stared at her through a mat of sand. "Of course I'm alive," he said gruffly. "Why shouldn't I be?"

"I thought you were dead," she babbled.

Using his elbow, he propped himself up to a sitting position. "You're crying," he said, reaching out a finger to caress the wet stains on her cheek. "I thought you couldn't cry."

"Me, too." She sniffled, grinning. "Guess I was wrong."

"Come here," he said gruffly, and clasped her to him.

Curling her head against his chest, she sobbed while he gently kissed her forehead and brushed soft tendrils of copper-colored hair from her face.

"I was so scared." She hiccuped.

"Shh," he soothed. "Everything's going to be all right."

"I lied to you, Dan. I lashed out and hurt you to protect my own emotions. I was so wrong."

"It's okay, sweetheart. I understand."

For several minutes he sat rocking her in his arms, bonding with her, absorbing her essence into his very marrow. An incredible peace enveloped him. Despite the storm, the lost horses and his injury, Dan experienced a profound sense of rightness. Things were as they should be, he and Raleigh together again. By the time her small body stopped trembling, the wind had quieted from gale to gust.

"We need to get you to the hospital," she said, wiping her mud-streaked face.

"I'm fine."

"Well, I'm not taking any chances," she declared, pushing away from him and standing. "Come on." She held out her hand and he took it, letting her help him to his feet.

"We're going to have to ride double," she said, waving a hand at Sunny.

"And bareback, too," Dan observed.

After Sunny put up an initial resistance at accommodating two riders, they eventually made it astride the reluctant mare. Dan rode in front, Raleigh behind, her thin arms wrapped securely around his waist, her cheek pressed against his back. He thrilled at the heavenly sensation.

"What about the horses?" Dan asked. "They all escaped from the corral."

"Forget them," she said. "Your health is more important than they are."

Her words surprised him. Could she really care more for him than the horses she adored?

They traveled through the gradually diminishing wind, Dan's brain swirling with thoughts. His head hurt, but he didn't mind. Raleigh was back, and that was all that mattered. He couldn't wait to get her alone someplace quiet.

The thought fueled him with unexpected energy, dispelling his aching weariness.

Sunny stumbled, lost her balance and slipped on the rocky surface. They lurched forward as the mare's back hoof caught her front. Dan heard the ping of metal striking stone. The mare staggered, limping.

"What happened?" Dan asked.

"She threw a shoe on these rocks." Raleigh sighed. "We'll have to walk the rest of the way, and I'll have to reshoe her when we get back."

"Can't it wait until morning?"

Raleigh shook her head. "Poor Sunny is so shallow footed, she can't manage long without being shod."

The storm had finally ended. Hand in hand, Dan and Raleigh plodded back to the ranch. Chester trotted along beside them, while Sunny limped behind. They wandered for many minutes and just when Dan feared they might be lost, he saw lights from the farmhouse glowing through the foggy darkness.

As they drew closer to the house, Dan could make out the shadowy shapes of Pete and his parents clambering down the front steps toward them.

"My folks are here," he told Raleigh, his voice raspy. "Be prepared for anything."

This is it, he thought, bracing himself. The big, father-son showdown. He knew this moment was inevitable, had been dreading it all week, but it was about time he took a stand and proved to his father, once and for all, that he was his own man.

"Daniel!" his mother cried, looking properly chic in a tailored pantsuit and understated gold jewelry, her frosted hair perfectly coiffed. She scurried across the yard and threw her arms around his neck. "Oh, my poor baby, are you all right?"

"Mother, I'm fine."

"But you're bleeding," she protested, her finger lightly stroking his wounded temple.

Dan stiffened and moved out of his mother's embrace. He refused to get sucked into that baby-of-the-family role again. Holding his head high, Dan locked eyes with his father. Squaring his shoulders, he stepped forward and thrust out his hand. It was now or never.

"Hello, Dad. Welcome to my home."

"Hello, son."

They stood a moment like two warriors, proud and strong. Neither wanting to be the first to look away, to back down.

Dan could feel the tense undercurrent flowing between them. What did his father think? Dan steeled himself for the obligatory put-down. Whatever the old man dished out, he could take.

Turning, Dan held out his arm to Raleigh. In an instant, she plastered herself to his side, her chin jutting forward defiantly as she eyed Bill McClintock.

"Mom, Dad, I want you to meet somebody special. This is Raleigh Travers, my farrier and friend. Raleigh, these are my parents, Bill and Marcia McClintock."

"How do you do, little lady?" Bill McClintock said.

"Nice to meet you," Marcia murmured.

Raleigh stepped up, shook both their hands, then allowed Dan to fold her into his arm once more.

Bill McClintock sank his hands on his hips and surveyed the shambles around them. Violent wind had ripped the corral gate off its hinges, sand lay in drifting piles, equipment was overturned, litter and debris clung to the fencerow.

"So," Bill McClintock said slowly, "this is the infamous dude ranch."

"Yes," Dan said proudly. "This is my ranch."

Raleigh laced her fingers through Dan's, giving him strength to face the man who'd controlled him all his life. Dan braced himself, prepared for a fight.

"Your ranch hand tells me you've misplaced a few horses," his father said, nodding in Pete's direction. "Tell me, son, is that standard operating procedure around here?"

"In case you haven't noticed, *sir,* there was a severe sandstorm tonight." Dan gritted his teeth and mentally counted to ten.

"You losing money on this venture?" His father shifted his weight but never dropped his gaze.

"Bill," his mother interceded. "I don't think this is the time. Dan needs medical attention for that gash on his forehead."

Bill McClintock raised a palm. "If Dan had stayed in the family business where he belonged, none of this would have happened. You'd think by now the boy would have learned to obey his parents."

"Now, Bill, Dan's always been a dreamer," his mother said in excuse.

Dan smiled, feeling strangely calm. *This* insecure bully was the man he'd feared all his life? Well, he wasn't a boy any longer and he refused to bow down to his father's demands.

"I gave you enough rope. Have you hung yourself yet, son? Are you ready to give up this nonsense and come back home?"

"No, Dad, I'm not. Clyde is my home now."

"Still have your heart set on playing cowboy?" Bill McClintock stuck his thumbs through his belt loops and gave Dan his best intimidating stare.

"You're jealous because I'm making it on my own," Dan challenged. "Admit it."

"You call this disaster, making it?" His father swung his arm at the mess surrounding them.

"I don't believe this!" Raleigh shouted, springing in front of Bill McClintock, her wiry legs cocked in the stance of a gunfighter, her waitress uniform pulling tight across her thighs. "Dan could have died tonight and all you care about is getting the upper hand."

"I beg your pardon, young lady." His father raised an eyebrow, looked from Raleigh to Dan and back again.

Admiration for his scrappy redhead swelled in Dan's heart. He grinned. She must love him to stand up for him like this, hanging tough with Bill McClintock.

"Raleigh," Dan admonished, wanting to deal with his dad on his terms. "I appreciate your concern, but this is my battle and I'll thank you to stay out of it."

"I just couldn't stand by and let him cut you down like that."

"Raleigh, please let me handle this." Dan raised an eyebrow.

She flicked her braid over her shoulder and gave him a haughty look. "Fine. If that's the way you want it. I'll be in the barn, attending to Sunny."

She stalked away, leading the mare behind her. Dan knew he'd ticked her off, but he realized he had plenty of time to make things up to her once he'd settled things with his father.

Pete mumbled something and took off after Raleigh, leaving Dan alone with his parents.

"Dad," he said once Pete and Raleigh were out of earshot. "I had hoped you'd come here to support my efforts to forge my own life. I'd think you'd want at least one son who was self-sufficient."

"Well, I—I," Bill McClintock stammered. Suddenly he didn't look so big and tough.

"I thought maybe we could bury the hatchet and face each other as equals. But if you can't do that, then I suggest you go back to Dallas." Dan stood as solid and steady as a hundred-year-old oak tree, no longer pliable to his father's demanding wishes.

"Danny, you don't mean that," his mother said.

"Yes, he does," Bill McClintock growled.

"And another thing," Dan said, knowing his words might alienate him from his father forever. "I'm going to marry that feisty girl, if she'll have me. So you better get used to the idea of people standing up to you, Dad. Raleigh doesn't take guff off anybody, including me."

To Dan's amazement, his father's face broke into a big grin. "By gum, Marcia," he hooted. "Our Dan's grown up at last."

Adrenaline pumped through Dan's body as he strode toward the barn. He felt good. Damn good. He'd faced his father and won.

And Raleigh had come home. Yes, home. He wanted to shout, to celebrate. Because both of them belonged here, on this ranch, on this land. Since she and Caleb had moved out, the place was like a morgue, cold, sterile, devoid of life.

But now Raleigh was back, with her special brand of verve. Love for her filled his very lungs as he inhaled sharp, musty air. He couldn't wait to propose to Raleigh, to hold her in his arms, to kiss those sweet strawberry lips.

His stomach tightened at the thought. He had to make her his wife, no matter what efforts might be required, because he loved her with every ounce of his being, with every breath he took. If she needed more time, then so be it. He had a lifetime to give.

Raleigh Jean Travers needed a man like him. A man who could show her the whimsical side of life. A man patiently willing to chip past her defenses. A man to help heal her broken heart. She needed him badly and, oh, how he needed her.

Almost running, Dan banged into the barn, his pulse pounding a mad tattoo.

Pete was in a stall, holding Sunny's head while Raleigh stooped over, her farrier's apron strapped around her pink uniform, the mare's hoof clenched between her legs, a rasp in her hand.

What a woman, Dan thought, his chest inflating with pride at the sight of her. She was brave, honest, hardworking. Strong, good and virtuous. She'd lived through adversity and survived victorious every time. What more could a man ask for in a helpmate, a lover?

"Raleigh," Dan called.

Slowly she raised her head.

"We've got to talk."

Pete stood, grinning like a fool. He dusted his hands on the seat of his pants. "That's my exit cue," he said.

"Where you going, Pete?" Raleigh asked, her heart leaping against her rib cage. "We're shoeing Sunny."

"It'll keep till tomorrow," Pete said, and slipped out the side door.

Leaving her alone with Dan.

When she'd first come back to the ranch, she'd been ready to declare her love to Dan, but now, after the storm and the episode with his parents, all her old doubts came rushing back. Did she truly dare to get involved again?

"I'm sorry if I insulted you back there in front of my parents, that wasn't my intention," he said.

She shrugged. "No offense taken."

Dan stepped closer, intently studying her in the glare from the bare bulb, that sweet pixie face with the sad gray eyes. How he longed to replace that sadness with joy.

"It was a personal thing between me and my father."

"I understand."

"I also want to thank you for saving my life tonight."

"You're welcome." She rocked back on her heels and stared at her toes. She pulled a shy, wry smile.

Dan's heart overflowed with hope. "Was there a reason you came back tonight?" His gaze never left her face. He wanted to absorb every nuance, decipher every emotion she experienced.

"I..."

"Look at me, Raleigh."

She raised her chin. "I came to tell you I lied."

"About what?" He inched closer until he stood a mere breath away.

"When I said I didn't love you. I tried not to love you, I really did, but it just didn't work."

"I'm so glad," he whispered.

"Fay told me how my pa broke her heart because he couldn't get over my mother, and I realized I was doing the very same thing to you. I've been hiding from life, denying your love because I didn't have the courage to risk losing you."

"Life's full of risk, Raleigh, but true love is worth any gamble."

"How can you be sure?"

A glint of metal caught Dan's eye. The horseshoe glistened.

He plucked it from the wooden frame. "I always heard these things were lucky. Do you suppose that's true?"

Raleigh shrugged.

"Well, I know they're lucky, because horseshoes are what brought you to me. You have faith in horseshoes, Raleigh, don't you?"

"Yes, I guess so."

"Then as long as we've got horseshoes, we've got good luck."

"Can I count on that?" she asked.

"You can count on me, darling," he said, and held his arms open wide.

"Oh, Dan." She dropped the rasp on the floor and, standing on tiptoe, wrapped her arms around his neck. She buried her face in his chest, relishing the pleasure of his embrace. It felt as if she'd just stepped from the deepest Arctic cold to a warm welcoming fire.

Dan tilted her chin up and stared down into her eyes. Then he angled his head and kissed her rich, strawberry-colored lips, slow, sweet and generous. With rising need, he placed kisses on her eyelids, cheeks, nose, only to return to her mouth again and again, and drink her sweet nectar.

Raleigh kissed him back hard and passionate, marveling at the intense sparking their coming together generated.

"Ah, sweetheart," he moaned, lifting her off the floor and pressing her to him. "I don't know how I've lived so long without you."

He curved one hand under her bottom, the other clutched her waist. She felt his body trembling with need, a need that matched her own.

What had she been missing all these long lonely years? Raleigh wondered with a sigh. Now she would find out—

with her sexy dude ranch owner to heat up the empty nights.

"I've got a confession to make," he said, tugging his lips from hers.

"Oh?" She arched an eyebrow.

"I invited my parents to our wedding."

"What?"

"That means you're going to have to agree to marry me so I can save face."

"And if I say no?" She smiled.

"Then I'll just have to kiss you until you change your mind." His mouth captured hers one more time before he set her on the floor. Her giggle of pleasure touched him as nothing else could have.

"Say yes," he prodded, leaning over to nibble at her ear.

"Hmm," she said. "What about Caleb?"

"I love you. I love Caleb. I want us to be a real family." His lips seared the hollow of her neck. Raleigh arched her neck and moaned.

"Say yes," he teased.

"You sure about this?"

"Of course, I'm sure." His mouth traced her chin. "I love you, Raleigh."

"I love you, too," she admitted, unbridled happiness flooding her body.

"And you'll marry me?"

Love. Marriage. Commitment. Suddenly everything she thought lost was within her grasp if only she had the guts to reach out and take it.

"Marrying you would be a great honor, Daniel J. McClintock."

"Oh, honey, the future's gonna be great. We're an unbeatable team, you and I," Dan whispered, his lips brushing her ears. "Together we're going to create the best dude ranch in West Texas."

"I thought you liked to dream big," Raleigh teased. "How about the best dude ranch in the whole U.S.A.?"

"Raleigh Jean Travers," he said. "You've got yourself a deal."

Epilogue

Dan looked out over his ranch and smiled. His beloved dream had finally come true. And here he was, sitting with his father on the patio, assessing the scene before them in an easy camaraderie they'd never before shared.

Two dozen cars crowded the freshly paved parking lot. A gaggle of squealing children splashed happily in the restored swimming pool. Vivid roses flourished in the flower garden Raleigh had planted.

Laughter sounded from several couples playing mixed doubles on the tennis court. A few old men tossed horseshoes on the lush green lawn. In the pasture, several city slickers struggled bravely to stay astride their spirited mounts. Next to the barn, Caleb and Pete were setting up picnic tables, preparing for the barn dance later that evening.

Dan took a deep breath and counted his many blessings.

"Well, son, I have to hand it to you. I never thought you'd accomplish this." Bill McClintock grinned at his son and rattled the ice in his tea glass. "The ranch is splendid. Couldn't have done a better job myself."

His father's words made him proud. "It takes a big man to admit when he's wrong, Dad. Thank you."

"I did a lot of things wrong with you boys. Wouldn't let you cut loose and do things your own way. When you tried, I belittled you. I hurt you, and I'm sorry."

"It's okay, Dad." Dan placed a hand on his father's shoulder. "Everyone makes mistakes."

Bill McClintock winked. "Wait until you have children of your own. Then you'll see how hard it is not to interfere in their lives."

Raleigh and his mother emerged from the house, joining them on the patio.

"Hi," Raleigh said, kissing Dan's cheek. Her feet were bare and she wore cutoff blue jeans.

"Hi, yourself." Playfully he tugged her braid.

She wrapped her arms around his waist and smiled at him. Dan marveled at the change in his bride. During the six months they'd been married, she'd blossomed before his very eyes.

Gone was the old, insecure, quick-tempered Raleigh and in her place stood a serene, easygoing young woman. She'd learned to funnel her explosive, passionate nature into lovemaking instead of arguing.

Dan smiled. No man could have asked for a better wife. She ran the ranch like an experienced business manager, while he handled the publicity and hosting aspects. They made an unstoppable team.

Gazing down at her, pride welled in his chest. With the dude ranch doing a booming trade and Raleigh at his side, what more could he ask for?

"Come on, dear, let's take a walk." Marcia McClintock linked arms with her husband.

"What for?" Bill McClintock grumbled. "I just got comfortable."

Marcia elbowed him. "Now, Bill, remember what we discussed."

"Okay, I get the picture." Dan's father set his empty glass on the table. "Let's go for a walk and you can tell me what I did wrong this time."

Dan chuckled, watching his parents head off toward the stables. One good thing had come from breaking free of his family's influence, he and his father had never been so close. The old animosity between them had dissipated completely.

"What was that all about?" Dan asked, moving over to sit on the porch swing and drawing Raleigh onto his lap.

Shyly, she ducked her head. "Your mom thinks it's time you and I had a private talk."

"Talk? I'd rather kiss." Dan caught her bottom lip between his teeth.

"Dan, not here. The ranch is full of guests." She waved a hand at the conglomeration of people enjoying themselves in the spring sun.

"They'll never notice."

She curled into the curve of his arm. "Well, I guess we better catch impromptu kisses where we can, 'cause later there'll be lots of interruptions."

As if on cue, Chester, followed by his new mate, Miss Kitty, and their three pups, loped up the steps looking for pats and scratches.

Raleigh leaned over and rubbed Chester's head. "Yep, handing out affection takes up lots of time."

"Stop being cryptic," Dan told her, lightly tickling her ribs. "What are you talking about?"

"Two a.m. feedings, Daddy."

"What?" Dan's eyes widened, his mouth fell open. Raleigh giggled.

"I...we...you're p-pregnant?" he stammered.

"We're having a baby."

"Oh, my gosh." His hands trembled. "When?"

"Not until December. I'm just two and a half months along. Perfect timing. The baby will be born during the winter lull."

Dan patted her tummy. "No wonder you look a little rounded. I thought it was my good cooking putting the weight on you."

"You're happy about this, aren't you?" A worried frown crossed her face. She traced a finger along his lips.

"Of course, I'm happy. Just surprised, that's all."

Raleigh blushed. "It's not like I wasn't exposed. Your mother guessed. She cornered me the minute they arrived."

Dan recalled Raleigh's old fears of intimacy—fears that had required a raging sandstorm to break down her carefully constructed defenses. Would she be so terrified of losing the baby she might resort to her old coping mechanisms, shutting him out, turning him away, taking refuge in stubbornness and anger?

"Are you scared?" he whispered, squeezing her tightly.

"Not as long as you're here with me. Together, we can do anything." She snuggled against him.

"Oh, Raleigh." He sighed. "Our life is going to be so good."

"I was hoping you'd say that."

"How do you feel?"

"Wonderful," she said. "Just like I do every time you make love to me. Making love and babies is the best way I know to dispel old ghosts."

"What an excellent idea," Dan said, cradling her in his arms. He stood and headed for the back door.

"Hey." She laughed. "What are you doing?"

"Becoming a certified ghostbuster." And with that, Dan whisked her into the house, carried her upstairs and did his best to ensure a very happy future.

* * * * *

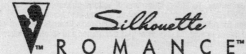

Silhouette ROMANCE™

COMING NEXT MONTH

MILLION DOLLAR SWEEPSTAKES (III)

No purchase necessary. To enter, follow the directions published. Method of entry may vary. For eligibility, entries must be received no later than March 31, 1996. No liability is assumed for printing errors, lost, late or misdirected entries. Odds of winning are determined by the number of eligible entries distributed and received. Prizewinners will be determined no later than June 30, 1996.

Sweepstakes open to residents of the U.S. (except Puerto Rico), Canada, Europe and Taiwan who are 18 years of age or older. All applicable laws and regulations apply. Sweepstakes offer void wherever prohibited by law. Values of all prizes are in U.S. currency. This sweepstakes is presented by Torstar Corp., its subsidiaries and affiliates, in conjunction with book, merchandise and/or product offerings. For a copy of the Official Rules send a self-addressed, stamped envelope (WA residents need not affix return postage) to: MILLION DOLLAR SWEEPSTAKES (III) Rules, P.O. Box 4573, Blair, NE 68009, USA.

EXTRA BONUS PRIZE DRAWING

No purchase necessary. The Extra Bonus Prize will be awarded in a random drawing to be conducted no later than 5/30/96 from among all entries received. To qualify, entries must be received by 3/31/96 and comply with published directions. Drawing open to residents of the U.S. (except Puerto Rico), Canada, Europe and Taiwan who are 18 years of age or older. All applicable laws and regulations apply; offer void wherever prohibited by law. Odds of winning are dependent upon number of eligible entries received. Prize is valued in U.S. currency. The offer is presented by Torstar Corp., its subsidiaries and affiliates in conjunction with book, merchandise and/or product offering. For a copy of the Official Rules governing this sweepstakes, send a self-addressed, stamped envelope (WA residents need not affix return postage) to: Extra Bonus Prize Drawing Rules, P.O. Box 4590, Blair, NE 68009, USA.

He's Too Hot To Handle...but she can take a little heat.

SILHOUETTE
Summer Sizzlers

This summer don't be left in the cold, join Silhouette for the hottest Summer Sizzlers collection. The perfect summer read, on the beach or while vacationing, Summer Sizzlers features sexy heroes who are "Too Hot To Handle." This collection of three new stories is written by bestselling authors Mary Lynn Baxter, Ann Major and Laura Parker.

Available this July wherever Silhouette books are sold.

HE'S MORE THAN A MAN,
HE'S ONE OF OUR

THE WOMEN IN JOE SULLIVAN'S LIFE
Marie Ferrarella

Joe Sullivan had enough on his mind with three small nieces to raise. He didn't have time for a relationship! But Joe couldn't deny the attraction he felt for Maggie McGuire, or the way this compelling woman cared about his sweet little girls. Maybe Maggie needed to love these little girls as much as he needed her, but it would take some convincing....

COMING IN AUGUST FROM

SOMETIMES BIG SURPRISES
COME IN SMALL PACKAGES!

BABY TALK
Julianna Morris

Cassie Cavannaugh wanted a baby, without the complications of an affair. But somehow she couldn't forget sexy Jake O'Connor, or the idea that he could father her child. Jake was handsome, headstrong, unpredictable...and nothing but trouble. But every time she got close to Jake, playing it smart seemed a losing battle....

Coming in August 1995 from

Silhouette ROMANCE™

BOJ3

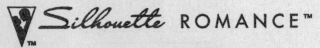

Silhouette ROMANCE™

is proud to present

The spirit of the West—and the magic of romance! Saddle up and get ready to fall in love Western-style with the fourth installment of WRANGLERS & LACE. Available in August with:

Cowboy for Hire
by Dorsey Kelley

Benton Murray was a cowboy with secrets—and now the former rodeo hero only wanted to forget the past. Then spirited Kate Monahan came to him with big plans for her own championship. All she wanted was someone to rein in her natural talent. And soon Benton was finding it difficult to deny her the help she needed—or the passion he felt for her!

Wranglers & Lace: Hard to tame—impossible to resist—these cowboys meet their match.

As a Privileged Woman, you'll be entitled to all these Free Benefits. And Free Gifts, too.

To thank you for buying our books, we've designed an exclusive FREE program called *PAGES & PRIVILEGES*™. You can enroll with just one Proof of Purchase, and get the kind of luxuries that, until now, you could only read about.

Big HOTEL DISCOUNTS

A privileged woman stays in the finest hotels. And so can you—at up to 60% off! Imagine standing in a hotel check-in line and watching as the guest in front of you pays $150 for the same room that's only costing you $60. Your *Pages & Privileges* discounts are good at Sheraton, Marriott, Best Western, Hyatt and thousands of other fine hotels all over the U.S., Canada and Europe.

Free DISCOUNT TRAVEL SERVICE

A privileged woman is always jetting to romantic places. When you fly, just make one phone call for the lowest published airfare at time of booking—or double the difference back! PLUS—

you'll get a $25 voucher to use the first time you book a flight AND 5% cash back on every ticket you buy thereafter through the travel service!

SR-PP3A

FREE GIFTS!

A privileged woman is always getting wonderful gifts.
Luxuriate in rich fragrances that will stir your senses (and his). This gift-boxed assortment of fine perfumes includes three popular scents, each in a beautiful designer bottle. <u>Truly Lace</u>...This luxurious fragrance unveils your sensuous side. <u>L'Effleur</u>...discover the romance of the Victorian era with this soft floral. <u>Muguet des bois</u>...a single note floral of singular beauty.

FREE INSIDER TIPS LETTER

A privileged woman is always informed. And you'll be, too, with our free letter full of fascinating information and sneak previews of upcoming books.

MORE GREAT GIFTS & BENEFITS TO COME

A privileged woman always has a lot to look forward to. And so will you. You get all these wonderful FREE gifts and benefits now with only one purchase...and there are no additional purchases required. However, each additional retail purchase of Harlequin and Silhouette books brings you a step closer to even more great FREE benefits like half-price movie tickets... and even more FREE gifts.

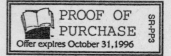

L'Effleur...This basketful of romance lets you discover L'Effleur from head to toe, heart to home.

Truly Lace...
A basket spun with the sensuous luxuries of Truly Lace, including Dusting Powder in a reusable satin and lace covered box.

Complete the Enrollment Form in the front of this book and mail it with this Proof of Purchase.